Mold and Marriage

Love's Infestation Series #1

Sophie Dawson

May your life be a story
in faithful living.

~~~~~

Sophie Dawson

Dedication

This book was started several years ago just before I took some time of to enjoy my granddaughter, Jady, during her pre-school years. Now that she's occupied more of her time I've come back to the writing God has planned for me to do. This book is dedicated, first to Him and second to her.

Prologue

"Oh no, look at that!"

Dr. Mark Jenner turned from looking at the patient lying in the hospital bed to the television on the wall. There was a news bulletin and, though the sound was muted, they could see there had been an explosion in one of the downtown high-rises.

"Turn up the sound," Mark said.

"We don't have many details as of this time as the police, fire and rescue personnel are just arriving. The KRTV studios are in the next block so we heard and felt the explosion. As you can see the entire front of the Dressler Building has suffered extension damage to the first three floors. We have no idea how many people have been injured or killed, nor do we know what or who caused the explosion."

The announcer paused, looking off camera for a moment.

"I've been instructed to move so the rescue vehicles can approach. We'll keep you appraised of this developing situation as soon as we know more. This is Kelly Miller reporting for KRTV."

Mark looked back at the man whom he had been giving discharge instructions to.

"Holy cow," the man said. "That looks bad."

Mark's phone cheeped. He drew it from the pocket of his lab coat. The text read, *All physicians to the ED stat. Explosion with multiple casualties.*

"I need to go. They're bringing the injured here. A nurse will be in shortly to finish with the instructions, then they'll spring you from this joint." Mark patted the elderly man on the arm in farewell and left the room.

He jogged down the hall and called, "Keith, hold the elevator." The surgeon he often worked with stood in the opening and stepped in as Mark passed into the car.

"Did you see the news flash?" Mark asked. He began buttoning his coat. He didn't want it to get in the way as he worked on a patient.

"No, just the text." Keith punched the button to the first floor.

"Explosion at the Dressler Building. The entire front for three floors is badly damaged. There will be a lot of casualties."

The door opened and Mark and Keith got off and hurried to toward the emergency department. Several nurses were speaking with people waiting to be seen. Some were being referred to the medical clinic down the street, explaining the influx of trauma patients and the extended wait time that would result for less severe cases.

Mark slashed his identification card through the

locking mechanism and the doors opened. They went in and over to the radio center. Several operators were speaking with EMT's on the scene and typing notes into their computers.

Mark and Keith looked at each other listening to the chatter and getting an idea of the types of injuries that would be coming in. Three more doctors came through the doors and stood nearby doing the same thing.

Several people had already been pronounced dead at the scene. Mark gritted his teeth. He'd known just from seeing the destruction to the building that there had to be fatalities but never even having a chance to try to save the lives bothered him.

"ETA three minutes on two ambulances," the head radio operator said. "In first female, mid-twenties, burns and shrapnel from glass and metal to her back. Multiple internal injuries from impact with possibly a parking meter and parked car."

"I'll take that," said Mark. "Which room?"

"Trauma three. It's set up for burns." The operator began reciting the details of the patient coming in the second vehicle as Mark walked toward the ambulance bay to meet it.

Even though the day was cold, he went outside to wait. The area always smelled of gas fumes. It didn't take long. The scream of the siren came first, then the flash of red lights. As soon as the ambulance stopped in the bay Mark pulled its door open allowing the crewman to jump down and begin to pull the gurney from the truck.

"Multiple second degree burns to her back and

extremities. Possible fracture to thoracic vertebra. Shrapnel type wounds to the same." He continued outlining the injuries and vital stats as they jogged toward Trauma Room Three pulling the gurney along.

It just might be a miracle if this young woman lived, Mark thought. As it was she would have a long, hard recovery if she managed to pull through. He began praying in the back of his mind as he issued orders to the staff gathered in the room.

Soon her clothing, what hadn't been shredded in the blast, was cut off and multiple IV's had been started. She was lying on her stomach as the damage to her back was extensive and needed treatment first. Mark ordered blood-work and X-rays, then stepped back to allow the portable machine into the room. He surveyed her back, arms and legs.

He picked up the telephone and called the university. The burns and cuts might benefit from the experimental skin gun that was awaiting FDA approval. It was a miraculous new machine that used stem cells to treat burns.

After the X-rays were complete the young woman, Kyria Metcalf, was surrounded once again by nurses and Mark gave instructions on how he wanted her treatment to proceed. Keith came in saying his patient had expired and he wanted to know if he was needed before the next ones arrived.

Just then Kyria jerked and began thrashing and groaning in pain. As those gathered around the bed touched her to stop her movements she began screaming.

"We need her sedated, stat," Mark shouted giving orders for the anesthetic to be administered. Within a few moments she calmed and went still.

~~~~~

Mark rubbed a weary hand down his face as he reviewed the reports of the cases he'd handled of the explosion victims. His most serious case was that of Kyria Metcalf. He still wasn't sure if she would survive or not. She was a very damaged young woman.

He looked at her personal information. She was twenty-six. If she lived she'd still be in the hospital on her birthday. She might even spend it in the drug induced coma they had placed her in. It was next week after all.

CHAPTER ONE

Approximately Five Weeks Later

"None of the green floor tiles got up and walked away during the night. That's good. Thirty-four, thirty-five, thirty-six. Now the blue ones." Kyria Metcalf began counting at the top left of her area of vision. It had become a ritual she did each morning; first the green, then blue, tan and finally the white. Anything to occupy her mind. No, not anything. She didn't want to think about what had brought her here.

The last she remembered was waving good-bye to Bert the security officer at the door. She had finished work early and left the office. They told her there had been an explosion. The police were still investigating, as were the FBI and Homeland Security. No one had claimed responsibility. The pain was always there to remind her.

Later in the morning the nurses would turn the Stryker Frame and put a remote in her hand so she could see the television. She would surf the channels trying to find something worthwhile to watch.

Pain rippled through her. Kyria ignored its ever-present annoyance. Maybe someday it would recede. From the moment she had awakened in the emergency room it had been a constant companion. The doctors said it would lessen with time.

"Good morning, Kyria. How are you? Stupid question, I know. It seems to simply come out without thought when I enter a room."

Kyria smiled. Dr. Mark Jenner often came in with some sort of a small joke or pun.

"So what's the number this morning?"

Kyria hated when they asked her to value her pain from one to ten. When pain is constant and barely lessens with the medicines injected into her IV, what was the point of asking?

"Your vitals look good."

A click and whir signaled that Dr. Jenner, or the nurse who was usually with him, was raising the bed. When it reached what Kyria thought was it's highest position she pasted a contented look on her face. Dr. Jenner, lying on his back, slid into her line of vision. The first time he had done so she'd startled badly. Now the movement of the bed and the sounds alerted her to his arrival.

"Why do you move the bed up so high? Surely you would fit under it if it was lower?"

Dr. Jenner laughed and lifted the sable colored hair from his forehead. "Do you see this scar? Before I made sure the beds were as high as they could go one decided to take a bite out of my head. Twelve stitches later and I make sure to raise it all the way up." His eyes, which matched his hair in color, sparkled making his handsome oval face even more friendly.

Kyria tried to laugh but it came out somewhat stilted. "Do you have many who need to lay like this?"

"Not often, but I always want be able to see them when I do. Especially when they are as pretty as this patient is." His grin told her the statement was sincere.

Warmth infused her face. How could he think she was pretty? She was lying face down on a Stryker Frame being suspended at various angles throughout the day and night. Only one of her individual injuries truly benefited from the frame but could have been treated without it. The combined total made it a necessity.

The explosion had brought her to the trauma center where she had woken in pain with what seemed a hundred doctors and nurses working on every part of her body. The pain had been excruciating, everywhere. Kyria hadn't been conscious very long when she blacked out again. She'd found out later that they had put her under so she wouldn't fight them.

When Kyria finally came to she found they had placed her in an induced coma for nearly ten days. One reason was so she wouldn't be in so much pain. The agony she'd been in at the time made her wonder how she could have been in more.

Dr. Jenner had sat beside her in ICU explaining all the damage her body had sustained. From her neck to her hips the skin of her back was a mass of second degree burns. The backs of her arms also were burned. She'd been wearing a felted slouch wool hat with her blonde streaked, light brown hair tucked up inside which had saved it and the back of her head from being burned. Also covering her back and that of her arms and legs were cuts from flying glass. It all needed to be dug out leaving her skin extremely damaged.

Internally she'd been a mess; damage to the liver, spleen and stomach. Four broken ribs, multiple compound fractures of her left arm, broken collar bone. Also several cracked vertebra. She felt fortunate that she didn't remember the explosion, sure she would have nightmares if she did.

"You never told me your pain number?"

"You know I hate when you ask that."

Dr. Jenner chuckled. "Yeah, I know, but the computer won't let me go on until I put a number in the box."

"Oh all right. How about five? Nice number right in the middle of the scale."

"Is that really your level or are you a junky just wanting more drugs? We call them frequent fliers in the ED."

"Yeah, it's a real level. Maybe more from being at this angle. I've been upside down most of the night."

"Well, let's put you on the carnival ride and turn you more upright."

The motor engaged and she was slowly turned until she was at slightly past upright taking the pressure off the straps across her shoulders and pelvis but not placing her weight onto her back.

"You'll be heading to X-ray today to see if you can get out of this contraption."

Against her will Kyria's eyes filled with tears. She closed them and the drops slid down her cheeks.

"Tears? Of joy I hope."

Kyria opened her eyes at the compassion in his voice, also present in his deep brown eyes. "I... I was just praying. As much as I want to get out of this thing, I want the pain to lessen. I'm so tired of it so I was asking God to let this ease the pain. That's all, just take away the pain."

"Well, that's specific, but doesn't show much faith in the God who created the universe. Let me pray for you."

"I... I don't know."

"Why not?"

"I suppose I don't want to hope more for than the minimum. That way whatever more He decides to bless me with will be wonderful. But— if He only gives me relief from pain I need to be satisfied. Paul had to bear it when God wouldn't take away his thorn in the flesh."

"True, but Scripture also says you have not because you ask not, and you don't receive because you don't believe."

"I didn't know you were a believer." Kyria lifted her arm and wiped at her face brushing some of her tears away.

"Guilty as charged. I couldn't watch the people suffer and possibly die without God to pour out my frustration, grief, and also praise to."

A wave of fear washed through her mind. She pushed it way. Fear was not of God. Kyria had clung to the thought since the explosion. Her entire life was at a standstill. What would it be like when she left the hospital? Would she have a job? Would she be able to work or would she simply be alone in her apartment with nothing to do?

A deep breath and a choice. "All right, pray what you want for me."

Dr. Mark Jenner scooted a little closer and she felt her hand being grasped. He looked directly into her eyes. Then he closed his.

"Yahweh, Yeshua, Holy Spirit. One of yours needs you. She needs you to help her believe that you are a god who wants to lavish your grace. Kyria is afraid. She fears to hope you will help in her healing. She fears continued pain and suffering. You, Lord, know of her suffering. You bore the pain for us.

"Father, I will do what I can through the blessings of the treatments you have revealed to us. You are the Great Healer and so we turn to you who can do all things and help us bear all things. We thank you for the promise of provision and mercy. In the precious name of your son, amen."

"Thank you, Dr. Jenner. I...I appreciate your taking your time to pray for me."

~~~~~

When Mark opened his eyes tears were dripping off her chin. He pulled a tissue from the box on the bedside table and wiped them from her face. He'd seen patients cry before, but none had ever affected him like Kyria did. She never complained. Rarely made requests of the nurses. Didn't seem upset with the lack of phone calls or visits from family or friends. Why did no one come? He'd never seen a patient without any visitors or calls. Maybe that was why he stopped in her room at times other than his morning and evening rounds.

"You're welcome, anytime. I'll be back this evening to let you know what the X-rays indicated and if you can be released from the grip of the metal monster."

"I'll be here. You won't have to go looking for me."

Mark thought her voice held a tinge of sadness along with the humor.

"One more thing," he said as he gave her hand squeeze. "I pray for you everyday. I do for all my patients."

"Thank you. I can use all the prayers I can get."

Mark looked at Kyria for a moment. He didn't say that he prayed for her more often than any other patient. Something about her simply kept his mind coming back to the large green eyes which hid so much.

CHAPTER TWO

Mark stood at the living room window of his newly purchased condo looking out at the lights of the city. The place had a wonderful layout; a master suite, two other bedrooms one of which he would use as an office, a great room with living, dining and kitchen area, and another bath and a half bath. The room arrangement had drawn him to the place as well as the low price. The decorating was a mess, however.

The picture windows in the great room were heavily covered with dark brocade drapes in black and red. Gloom started and progressed through the entry space. Black carpet, deep red and dark grey walls made the place feel closed in. It reminded him of a medieval castle or maybe the dungeon of one.

Taking a swig of his soda, Mark thought again, for what must have been the hundredth time, of Kyria's green eyes which spoke volumes of hope and fear. Tomorrow she would be in a regular hospital bed rather than the Stryker Frame. Her vertebra had healed enough to allow her to lie on her back in a body brace.

He marveled at how the skin on her back and limbs looked now. They had been covered with second degree burns and cuts. Several hours after Kyria had stabilized that first day her back had been sprayed with skin stem cells taken from an unburned area of her body. It seemed to Mark that the experimental stem-cell skin gun, as it was called, was a miracle from God. What used to take weeks or months for burns to heal into stiff painful scar tissue, could now heal with no scarring whatsoever in a matter of days.

But something more bothered him. Why did no one call or inquire about her? The nurses commented on it at change of shift. Never had there been a patient on the floor who'd had no one. Even if family couldn't come they would call. Many patients had multiple calls during the day.

Mark had asked if anyone ever called or came to visit Kyria. The Human Resources person from the interior design firm she worked for had called a couple of days after the explosion asking how long she would be unable to work. The other was from the superintendent of her apartment building saying he was taking care of her cats. Both calls were while Kyria was still in the drug induced coma. Neither had called again.

It seemed obvious to Mark that Kyria either had no family or wasn't close to them. This concerned him as a doctor as well as a compassionate person. She was going to need help and care after they released her from the hospital. Kyria had been in the Stryker Frame for nearly five weeks after she was brought out of the coma. She would be weak as a newborn kitten, barely able to take care of herself, let alone an apartment with the activities of daily living.

"Lord, how can I help her? She doesn't have anyone it seems. How lonely must she be?" Mark prayed. His parents lived a few hours away, as did his sister and three brothers. Each would come to see him if something like this happened, as he would if there was a family member in need. His mother would have stayed and helped until he was well. Always secure in his support system, it was foreign and frightening to him to think of not having family.

The door bell rang signaling the arrival of his pizza and he went to answer it knowing he would spend the evening thinking about Kyria and her situation. Tomorrow he had time and would see if he could find out more about her. He hoped to figure a way to help her.

~~~~~

Mark walked through the damaged lobby of the Dressler Building where the explosion happened. Construction was underway on the repairs. Seventeen people had been killed and many more wounded. Survival guilt would be another hurdle

Kyria would have to get past.

Scanning the white board that was temporarily replacing the directory of businesses, Mark located Kempfer Design. He'd gone over Kyria's medical record finding not only her employer but also her address. There was no one listed as an emergency contact. He hoped to find out something here. He sent up a prayer as he pressed the elevator button.

Kempfer Design was obviously a large firm since there was a receptionist who made a phone call when he stated his purpose. She indicated he wait until called. Mark wasn't accustomed to being kept waiting when he requested something He sat in the beautiful sitting area in a comfortable chair, his knee bouncing up and down.

"Dr. Jenner?"

Mark looked up and saw a middle aged man. "Yes," he said as he stood and approached, hand outstretched in greeting.

"Blaine Ditto, human relations, we'll talk in my office."

"Sandy tells me you came to discuss Kyria Metcalf," Blaine said once they were seated in his office. "What can I help you with? First, how is she doing?"

"Better, she's still in quite a bit of pain."

"We were all worried and the nurse was very gracious and reassured us she would live. I couldn't speak with her since I'm not family. I hope they told her we would keep Kyria's job open for her. She's one of the best young designers we have."

"I'm not sure. I'll be sure to tell her next time I see her." Mark was relieved Kyria at least had a job to return to. "What I've come to find out, if you can help me, is to find her next of kin. No one has been contacted in her family."

If the HR director was surprised that her physician came with this inquiry he didn't show it. "I can't give you the information, but maybe I can contact them for you. Let me see." Blaine searched in his computer while Mark looked on. "The emergency contact is Naylor & Burns Attorneys at Law. Nothing other than this. It's a law firm so I can give it to you. I'll write down the information."

Mark watched as Blaine wrote on a sticky note, wondering even more about Kyria's seeming aloneness. Only a law firm as emergency contact. He'd call as soon as he left.

The next morning Mark was at the nurse's station going through patient records on the computer when a clearing of throat broke into his concentration.

"Excuse me," a squat, silver haired man said. "I'm looking for Dr. Jenner."

Mark stood. "I'm Dr. Jenner."

"I'm Russell Naylor, you called my office yesterday about Kyria Metcalf. I was in court all day and didn't get back to the office until this morning."

A flood of relief larger than he had anticipated surged through him. Mark reached out a hand and said, "I'm very glad you've come. Let's go speak in private, shall we."

In silence they went into Mark's office closing the door. Mark indicated a chair for Mr. Naylor then seated himself behind his desk.

"How is Kyria? I was out of the country when the explosion happened and never knew she was involved."

"Are you family, Mr. Naylor?" Mark asked.

"No, but I have documents stating you can give information to me." He pulled the papers from his briefcase and handed them to Mark who looked them over.

"I'll have them scanned into her chart so you can call or visit."

"Thank you."

"Kyria is healing well, now. We had to keep her in a coma for over a week to help with the pain." Mark explained her condition and treatment from the time Kyria was brought to the ED until now. As he spoke the older man's affection and care for her was evident. Another wave of reassurance flowed through him. Why was this patient's situation so much more in the front of his mind than any other?

"I'd like to ask you a question now," Mark said when he was sure the man understood everything about Kyria's condition. "No one, not a family member or friend, has called or come the entire time she's been here. Is she all alone?"

Mr. Naylor cleared his throat. "Essentially, yes. Her parents are gone, as well as her grandparents. Her brother is, let me see, climbing Mt. Kilimanjaro right now, I think. I'm the person who handles the trusts for the family."

"Oh," was all Mark could think of to say. He wanted to ask more but knew the confidentiality of attorney client privilege was similar to that between patient and doctor. "Would you like to go see her?"

"By all means."

When they entered her room Mark said, "Hi Kyria."

"What are you doing back here? You were in about an hour ago and told me everything was going well."

"I just wanted to make sure you hadn't been bothering the nurses so much that they put you back into the metal monster."

Kyria's laugh was delightful and without a trace of sadness or fear.

"I've brought you a visitor."

Her entire body jerked at his statement.

"Hello, Kyria." Mr. Naylor's voice was tight with emotion as he stepped from behind Mark. "I'm sorry I didn't come sooner. I was out of the country and didn't know you'd been injured."

~~~~~

"Uncle Russ." Kyria's throat tightened as she tried to swallow the emotion which welled inside. She'd known he was out of the country at the time of the explosion and didn't know he was back. "Thank you for coming." She reached out a hand which was grasped and given a squeeze.

"I feel so guilty that I didn't know. I would have come sooner if I had."

She could hear it in his voice. "It's all right. I'm going to be fine. Please don't feel guilty." Kyria couldn't say more because of the lump in her throat so she squeezed his hand. He was the only link to her family. Not a real uncle, but a long time friend of the family, he'd been named the executor of the trusts which had been set up before her parents' deaths.

"I still wouldn't have known you were in the hospital unless the good doctor here hadn't tracked me down. I'm not sure what gyrations he had to go through to find me, but I'm very glad he did."

"Just doing what's best for my patient," Mark said.

CHAPTER THREE

Mark walked along the hospital corridor heading to Kyria's room. He couldn't seem to stay away. Some of his concern had been assuaged with Russ Naylor coming to visit her. At least she had one person. With her continued progress Kyria would soon be released. He swung into her room and smiled.

"Looking good, Kyria," he said. "I must say I'm glad you've been in the regular bed for a week now. Much easier on this old codger's back." He made a show of limping across the room holding his back.

"Sorry, Doc. I've got no sympathy for you." Kyria's eyes twinkled. "Whatever pain you might have is nothing compared to that of your patients."

"Ah, come on, just a wee smidgen? Some little bit for your handsome doctor?" Mark teased back.

"Handsome? I'd not noticed." She was rubbing her chin as if in contemplation. "You're passable, I guess."

Now he placed his hand on his chest staggering around as if wounded. "Shot down again. You wound me. I hope it's not mortal."

"Don't worry," she said flatly but with delight in her eyes. "You'll survive. I'm sure there are several nurses who will gladly stroke your damaged ego."

Mark sat on the edge of the bed. "You sure know how to knock a guy off his pedestal." His smile took any sting out of his words.

"God draws near to the humble..." She stressed the word

humble trying to keep from laughing.

"Oh all right. I'll be my glorious humble self." Mark chuckled when Kyria finally lost it and burst out laughing. Her laugh delighted him and he simply looked at her. Someone had helped her wash her hair which flowed around her shoulders in great waves of light brown and blonde. It had been kept in braids while she was on the Stryker Frame. Long dark lashes framed green eyes with golden specks. He took her hand in his. "It's good to hear you laugh."

Kyria smiled softly at him. "It's good to feel like laughing."

A knock caused Mark to pull his hand from hers and grab the stethoscope from around his neck. For some reason he was embarrassed being caught holding her hand.

"Kyria Metcalf?" Two men in black suits came into the room.

"Yes?" Kyria said.

"We're from Homeland Security and we have some questions for you about the explosion. I'm Mitch Howard, this is my partner Stewart Kendel." The men pulled out identification badges.

Mark looked at Kyria. She'd paled and was gripping the blanket with white knuckles. "Gentlemen, I know you need to question Ms. Metcalf, but remember she is still weak and can't be stressed."

"And you are?" Kendel asked.

"Dr. Mark Jenner, Kyria's physician and hospitalist." He held out his hand in greeting.

"I see." Kendel said as he jotted some notes on the pad he carried.

"Ms. Metcalf," said Howard. "I understand you exited the building just before the explosion. What do you remember about it?"

"Not much. I waved to Bert the security guard, then left the building and turned left heading to a cafe nearby. That's really all I remember."

Mark saw her jolt and studied her. She'd gone even whiter, putting a shaky hand to her face. He took her hand again.

"Bert was killed in the explosion, wasn't he?" Tears flooded her eyes and fell down her face. This time it was Kyria who pulled her hand away. She covered her face with both hands as sobs overtook her. "When they said seventeen dead I didn't relate that to Bert. Do you know who else was killed?" she asked when she could speak again.

"There's an official list. You can find it on the internet." Kendel said with no emotion.

"I think, since she doesn't remember anything else, this interview is done." Mark stood and faced the men.

Howard and Kendel looked at him. Mark knew if they pressed the issue he'd have to allow them to question her. Howard pulled a card from his pocket. "If you remember anything; a suspicious face, package, vehicle, anything call me at this number." He laid the card on the bedside table. "Any detail may help."

"I will." Kyria's voice was just above a whisper. Her eyes were wide and hollow looking.

Mark followed the men to the door which he closed behind them. Coming back to her bed, the distress was evident in her expression and body language. His heart constricted. This time when he sat on the bed he didn't hold her hand. Instead, he gathered her to him and held her as once again she broke down and wept.

~~~~~

Kyria was sitting in a large recliner looking at the tray of hospital food. She gently placed her fork down and pushed the table away. Hospital meatloaf, stewed tomatoes and jello just couldn't be faced. She hated jello and after what she'd realized today it looked even worse.

She couldn't believe Bert was dead. He'd been so sweet to her, talking to her everyday. Making sure she got a cab when the weather was bad even though her apartment was only five blocks away.

She'd brought him a huge tin of cookies last year for Christmas. In the bottom she'd placed an envelope with a more substantial gift. Kyria had known he wouldn't have taken the cash if she'd given it right to him.

What would his wife and three teenage children do now? She'd call Uncle Russ in the morning when she felt better and have him send them an anonymous gift from her trust fund, or her savings account. She didn't care. They needed it more than she did.

"Hey, beautiful. How about some grease?" Kyria looked up to see Dr. Jenner holding a bag and cardboard tray with two drinks. He smiled a hopeful smile. She knew he was trying to cheer her up.

She smiled knowing it didn't reach her eyes. "I can hear some veins clogging, but yeah."

Mark came over, set the bag on the table, and handed her the drinks. "I'll just get this yuck out of here." He took the supper tray and left the room quickly returning, pushing the door nearly closed behind him. "Nurse Gadsden is on duty tonight. We'll have to eat this quickly and get rid of the evidence. She doesn't approve of Micky D's."

"What are you still doing here? I thought you would have gone home by now." Kyria said as she looked into the bag. "What'd you get?"

"Pulling a double shift for a friend. Big juicy cheeseburgers, large fries, cookies and chocolate shakes."

Kyria laughed. "Grease, sugar and chocolate. What a wonderful meal."

Mark watched as she dug around in the bag. It seemed every emotion she had was expressed to the max. As he'd held her when she cried that afternoon he knew her heart was breaking for those who had died and the loved ones left behind. Now she was stuffing french fries in her mouth with joyous abandon.

"Hey, let me have some of those." Mark reached into the container and pulled several fries out while she batted at his hand.

"I thought you got these for me?" Kyria teased.

"Only half are for you. The other half are for me."

"There's another container in the bag. These are mine." She held the fries away from him.

"But yours might be better." He pretended to struggle for them.

"Stop, get your own. I haven't had real food since I got here."

"Okay, you win." Mark pulled fries and the burgers from the bag. He handed Kyria one of the burgers and settled in to eat his.

"Oh my, this is good." Kyria took another bite.

"Yeah, nothing like a big honkin' burger," Mark bit into his.

"Eh hem."

Mark turned to look at the door the burger still at his mouth. Kyria had a huge mouthful. Nurse Gadsden stood there with hands on her hips and a frown on her face.

"Yes, Ms. Gadsden? Is there something you need?" Mark asked as he chewed.

"I thought I would take the supper tray, but I see it's already gone."

"Yes, I thought Ms. Metcalf might like some outside food." He took a big bite of he burger.

"I see. At least I'll know where you are if you're needed, Dr. Jenner." She turned and left the room.

Mark and Kyria look at each other. Both had mouths full of cheeseburger. They covered their mouths as they fought not to laugh and spit it out.

"Busted," Mark said when he finally swallowed.

Kyria swallowed and laughed.

Mark wanted to lean forward and kiss her. What had brought that thought on? She was just a patient. She'd be leaving the hospital soon. The thought sobered him. He wanted her to be released, but didn't want not to see her again.

"Oh, that was so good. Thank you, Dr. Jenner." Kyria was leaning back in her chair with a satisfied grin. Mark again felt the pull to kiss her.

"Kyria," he started, then his cell phone rang. After taking the call he said, "Well, I've got to go. I'll see you tomorrow. I've gotten good reports on your physical therapy results. We'll start planning your release."

"That sounds wonderful. See you tomorrow. Sleep sweet."

"You, too." Mark left thinking he was glad he succumbed to his urge to bring her the fast food. He should keep things strictly professional between them. It was only the attraction of a pretty woman who needed him. Funny, it was usually the patient who was attracted to the doctor.

~~~~~

Kyria watched him leave, taking the trash with him, and sighed. He was just about six feet of lean muscle. Clean shaven with neatly trimmed hair. Very attractive to her way of thinking She could really fall for that guy. But she knew better. Patients had been attracted to their doctor or nurse for ages. Kyria wasn't going to waste time dreaming about a handsome, friendly, funny man she'd never see again once she left the hospital.

Nurse Gadsden came in with a frowning face and stood in front of her, hands in the pockets of her butterfly covered scrubs. "I'm only saying this for your own good. Be careful you don't think more of his attention than you should. I'd hate to see you moon over someone who'll forget about you in a couple of weeks."

Kyria smiled. "I was thinking the same thing. Thank you for caring enough to say something."

The frown turned into a startled 'O,' then into a grin. "You're welcome. Also, I know I was stern about the burgers and fries. It was more about protecting you from his attention. Dr. Jenner can be pretty charming when he wants. Now, how about we get you to the bathroom and ready for sleep?"

"Sounds good. I can't believe how tired I am sitting in this chair. I've spent so much time lying down the past month. I would have thought I'd be done sleeping."

"You've been inactive for so long it will make you weak. It'll take you a while to regain your strength," Ms. Gadsden said as she helped Kyria to the bathroom. "When you go home, you be sure to rest and slowly add to what you do or you'll end up back in the hospital."

Kyria thought that might be very good advice.

CHAPTER FOUR

Sitting in a wheel chair so she wouldn't have to walk through huge hospital to get to the entrance, Kyria looked around the room she'd stayed in for so long. She was finally going home. Anxiety and excitement warred within her. She longed to see the apartment she loved, but worried over her weakness.

It felt good to be in real clothes instead of hospital gowns. Her Uncle Russ had bought a purple fleece jogging outfit as well as underthings, purple and lime green tennis shoes and socks before he left the country on another business trip. Kyria wished he was here. It would be lonely knowing no one but the respite aide would be coming to visit. But she was used it. Being alone was as familiar as a favorite pair of sweat pants and shirt.

Physical therapy had worked with her so she could walk the distance from the building entrance to her apartment. A respite care aide had been hired to visit each day helping with cooking, shopping, laundry and other chores of daily living until Kyria had the strength and doctor's approval to do them for herself.

"Hey beautiful," Dr. Jenner's customary greeting made Kyria smile.

"Hey handsome."

"Thought I'd stop by to say farewell." He sat down on the rumpled bed.

"Thank you, I appreciate it. Thank you also for your great care and compassion. It helped tremendously."

"No thanks needed. You were a model patient."

They went on discussing follow up treatment. Then silence,

awkward and cumbersome, descended. They'd always been able to make light banter fill any space within a conversation. Now Mark sat with his hand fingering something in his pocket.

"Kyria, here's my business card with my home and cell on it. If you have any problems or need anything, please, give me a call." Mark pulled the card with the hand written numbers on the back from his lab coat pocket and handed it to her.

"Thank you."

"Really, I know you don't have much of a support system. Please, at least give my name to your doorman so if you do call I can get in the building."

"All right." Kyria cleared her throat. "My chariot driver will be here soon, and I don't want to keep you from your patients. Thank you again."

Mark looked at her. "Kyria, may I..." A code blue was announced over the intercom. "I need to leave. Don't forget your followup appointment in two weeks." Mark took her hand, quickly giving it a squeeze before he left the room.

Kyria closed her hand as if to capture the feel of his after Mark left. It was silly, she knew, but she did it anyway. She'd miss him and felt as if she was losing a friend.

"Well, young lady, are you ready to ride out of here?" A cheery older man entered the room. "I'm Dan, a volunteer pusher here at the hospital. Wheelchair pusher, not drugs." He laughed at his own joke.

"Hi, Dan. I'm more than ready." Kyria smiled up at the vigorous grey haired man dressed in khakis and polo shirt.

"Do you have all your belongings? I used to call it stuff, but my wife told me that was crass."

Smiling Kyria held up the large plastic bag with the articles from her purse, which had been ruined. "All here."

"Then let's go," Dan said as he began pushing her to a taxi waiting below.

~~~~~

Kyria paid the cab driver as Pete, the daytime doorman for her building, opened the car door. Then she stood on the sidewalk looking around. Nothing had changed in the neighborhood. Chet's Chinese was across the street. Nino's Pizzeria. Mi Casa

Mexican. Olive's Deli. All would deliver, thankfully. Mel's Market would, too.

"Welcome back, Ms. Metcalf. We've missed your smiling face around here. Was very sorry to hear you were involved in that explosion." Pete took the bag she was carrying then her arm, helping her into the lobby. "Do you have your key?"

"It's good to be back. It's been a rough couple of months. The key is in the bag. This is all that was left. Everything else was ruined."

Pete held up the bag with its meager contents and gave a low whistle. "Wish I could escort you clear up to your apartment, but I've got to stay here."

Kyria patted his arm. "I'm fine. Thank you for getting me this far." They'd arrived at the elevator. She pressed the up button. "Oh, I promised I'd tell you that Dr. Mark Jenner is to be allowed up if he comes. He won't, but I promised."

Pete's right eyebrow rose and he smiled. "So he wants to be sure to be permitted up. Sounds like he might just want to come and see you."

"No, he thinks I'm all alone and can't function for myself. He told me to call if I needed help. He doesn't know I have several doormen who will do anything I ask of them."

Pete laughed. "You've got that right, Ms. Metcalf."

"Also a respite care aide will be coming. I don't know her name, but she'll be coming tomorrow."

The elevator arrived and Kyria stepped in. Once the door closed she leaned against the wall. Thankfully, her apartment wasn't at the far end of the hall but nearer the elevator. She clutched her key as the elevator rose to her floor. Taking a fortifying breath, Kyria stepped into the hallway and slowly walked to her apartment.

Home, she was finally home. Kyria placed her keyring in a blown glass bowl and the bag on the counter separating the kitchen from the living room and walked to the sofa nearly collapsing onto its softness. Her knees were shaking. She raised a hand and looked at it. It was shaking, also. Kyria realized then how weak she truly was. She hadn't wanted the respite care aide but reluctantly agreed to it. Now she was glad the woman would come tomorrow to help.

Kyria looked around the room running her hand over her white leather sofa. The apartment was only one bedroom and small. She loved the soft white walls and light celery carpet. Comfortable blue chairs offered seating on the other side of a glass coffee table with a marble base. Light blue drapes framed the windows. Accents of celery, blue and tan were scattered throughout the room.

A quilt made from the same colors was folded on the back of the sofa. Kyria pulled it over her as she reclined and closed her eyes. Her last thought before she fell asleep was to call the building super in the morning and get Cece and Mini, her cats, back.

~~~~~

It was dark when she woke. Lights from the buildings viewed through the windows welcomed her as a familiar vista. Kyria got up and went into the kitchen. Opening the fridge she looked and closed the door again. Almost two months ago the food had been fresh. Now the milk was sour and vegetables and meat covered in grey fuzz. Swallowing, she turned away even more grateful the respite aide was coming in the morning.

A call to Mi Casa ensured she'd eat better than she had in a month. Thinking of the supper of burgers and fries Dr. Jenner had brought a few nights before, she smiled.

Kyria always thought of him as Dr. Jenner not wanting to think of him as she would like. Mark Jenner, handsome, funny, with warm brown eyes and hair that the covered a scar he'd gotten making sure he spoke to his patient's face rather than their back.

It would have been nice to have met him under different circumstances. Maybe at church or an event they'd both been invited to. Maybe they could have become friends. It was a vain hope.

The remains of the veggie enchiladas and rice were in the trash when Kyria went to bed wondering if she'd ever see the attractive Dr. Jenner again.

~~~~~

It was late when Mark finally left the hospital and got into his car to drive home. He'd not gotten the chance to truly say good bye to Kyria. It wasn't as if he made sure to give a special farewell to each of his patients. He didn't. He had wanted to speak with Kyria and the code blue came at just the wrong time. Lucky for him he had access to her records and could get her home address and phone number. It wasn't HIPPA compliant, but no one would know.

As friendly and easy going as Kyria appeared to be, Mark couldn't figure out why she didn't seem to have close friends who would have visited her. She had mourned the security guard who'd been killed in the blast, so he must have been a bit more than an acquaintance.

He knew of people who shunned friendships, but they were usually grumpy or standoffish. Kyria certainly wasn't either. She was, at the most, quiet when she was in pain. As her pain had lessened she had teased and joked with him and the nurses. Kyria had been a favorite of all the staff. They had spoken about how cooperative she'd been. How she seemed to try to smile through her pain and would always thank them for their care.

It simply didn't add up. Her personality was one which could draw people to her. She should be able to make friends easily. So why didn't she have any?

Mark pulled into the underground parking for his condo building. He was tired and hungry. He hoped there was something in his refrigerator. As he rode the elevator up an idea came to him. He could contact Kyria inquiring about her services in redecorating his condo. It certainly needed a makeover. Speaking to her about it was a legitimate excuse to call. He'd give her a few days to settle in at home, then he would call.

CHAPTER FIVE

"Hi, I'm Amisa Borrier," the respite aide, a smiling black woman, said when Kyria opened the door to her apartment.

"Come in. I'm Kyria Metcalf." She stepped back holding onto the door. Kyria couldn't believe how shaky her legs were. She'd gotten up and showered about a half hour ago and toasted a frozen waffle for breakfast.

Amisa walked in and took Kyria by the arm leading her to the sofa. "You sit right here. I'm going to look you over and then get to doing the things needing done. I'm an RN and could be working at a hospital or doctor's office. This gives me more flexibility with my kids. I can be there when they leave for school and when they get home.

"Now, you sit down here and cover up with this quilt. My, it's pretty, just like this room. Did you make the quilt?"

"No, I would like to try sometime though." Kyria stretched out and allowed Amisa to cover her. The nurse then opened her giant orange bag and pulled out a stethoscope, blood pressure cuff, digital thermometer and computer.

"I know it's a loud color but it holds everything I need and there's no hiding if the kids try to get into it. I've got three, ages five, eight and ten. Two boys and a girl. My husband, Tyron, is an electrician. We've been married twelve years. You don't have a temperature and your pulse is fine. Let me listen to your heart and lungs, will you?"

Kyria leaned forward and took deep breaths as Amisa listened, her long corn row braids falling over her shoulders even though they were pulled back in a scrunchy at her nape. As soon as the nurse was finished she began again with a stern expression. "It looks to me as if you've taken a shower with your hair wet like that. I want you to wait for me to come tomorrow before you bathe. I can't get into your apartment if you fall. I'm sure you'd be all right, but I need to be here. Yes, I know you'll be fine, but just to humor me. Please wait."

"Okay," Kyria said, feeling like a naughty child. Amisa patted her hand.

"It's frustrating, isn't it, being so weak. You'll get stronger sooner if you take it easy, yet push yourself just a little each day. Overdo and you'll set yourself back. Now that we have the medical stuff done, let's get to know one another and make a plan about today and the rest of the week."

The morning was spent doing just that. Amisa then ran down to Subway bringing back sandwiches and cookies. Kyria moaned with pleasure at each bite. After over two months, her mouth and stomach craved anything other than hospital food.

"This is so good, Amisa. Thank you for getting it."

Amisa laughed then went to answer a knock on the door. "Come in, come in. I'm sure Ms. Metcalf will loved to see you."

Kyria, lying on the sofa facing the windows rather than the door, turned to see who was coming in. Her face lit and she slowly rose going to greet Steve Baker the building super.

"Oh, I'm so glad to see you. Let me have the carrier, please." Her voice was nearly pleading.

"How about I put it on the sofa and you can greet your babies," Steve said. Mews sounded and two pair of golden eyes looked through the mesh.

Kyria unzipped the carrier as soon as they were settled and the cats tumbled out and into her lap. Tears came to her eyes as she hugged each one to her. Loud purrs emanated from the small bodies as they rubbed their heads against her. "Did you miss me as much as I missed you?"

"They sure enough did, Ms. Metcalf. For days they just sat in the window like they was looking for you to come for them and get them out of the mad house they'd been moved to."

"Mr. Baker, how many times have I asked you to call me

Kyria?" She shot a teasing stern glance at him.

"Same number I've asked you to all me Steve."

They both laughed, then Kyria introduced Amisa. After bringing the cats' food and litter box in, Steve left.

"What's wrong with that one?" Amisa asked, pointing to the grey longhaired tabby with very short legs.

"Mini is a standard Minuette. She's got short little legs. It's a relatively new breed; a mix between a Munchkin and a Persian. Cece is her sister but has long legs. I got her at a discount since she's tall."

"Never seen anything like Mini. She's cute though."

Just then Mini raised up on her back legs just like a prairie dog and looked at Amisa who laughed. "She's trying to look from a higher position. How funny."

The cats entertained them for a while as they climbed all over Kyria. Then they ran around the room and into other areas of the apartment getting reacquainted with their home. Pretty soon Kyria yawned. Even though she hadn't done much in the morning, her injured body needed rest. Amisa became a nurse again.

"You will go into your room and take a nap. I'll go and do the grocery shopping and make something for supper. Also, clean out that fridge. It's pretty gross."

"I looked yesterday, but just shut the door. I simply couldn't face it."

"That's what I'm here for. I'll just pitch it all and start fresh."

Soon Kyria was tucked in bed with her cats curled up close to her legs. It was so good to have them back.

Amisa was great company and very good help. She would be coming daily for a while helping Kyria as she gained her strength back. Kyria slipped into slumber wishing the cheery black woman could become a friend but knew it wasn't possible. Kyria didn't know how to make friends.

~~~~~

Amisa came either in the morning or afternoon each day for the next four. Then, over the weekend, an older aide came, did the bare minimum and left within an hour and a half. She obviously didn't like cats, sniffing in disgust at the first sight of them. Kyria was left to not only care for herself but also cook meals.

After the aid left on Saturday morning Kyria showered then went to the deli across the street. She planned to take her sandwich back to her apartment but by the time she had stood in line her legs were shaking, collarbone protested, ribs hurt and her back throbbed. She sat at one of the small tables and ate, not venturing home until her legs felt stronger. Then she crawled into bed, sleeping the rest of the afternoon.

Sunday was no better. Pizza she could have delivered, but no one would clean the cat litter but herself. The trash shoot was at the other end of the hallway. To Kyria, it seemed at least five miles long. The heavy door very nearly defeated her attempt to open it. Only a foot forced between it and the frame gave her victory instead of defeat. Her back protested and made its dislike of her activity evident throughout the afternoon and evening. Pain tablets let her sleep that night.

The phone ringing woke Kyria on Monday morning. She glanced at the clock on her bedside table as she fumbled for the phone. Six-thirty.

"Hello?"

"Kyria, this is Amisa. I'm not going to be able to come today. My kids and my husband have been throwing up all night. I don't want to bring it to you and I'm really needed at home."

"I'm sorry to hear that." Kyria really was. She'd been looking forward to Amisa's tender care for two days.

"I'll call the agency. I'm sure they could send someone. Maybe the aide who's been helping you over the weekend. She knows you and your case now."

Kyria thought fast. "Don't you worry. I'll take care of it. You just care for your children and husband and don't worry about me."

"I'm so sorry. I'll come back as soon as they're well."

"I know you are. You stay well and take care of your family. Bye."

Kyria lay looking up at the ceiling. Cece and Mini climbed onto her chest crying for breakfast. She stroked their soft fur. Twins, except for the length of their legs they butted their heads against her chin.

I'm not calling the agency. Let them think Amisa is here. I don't want the old cat hating lazy bat they sent. I'll get along until Amisa comes back. Deciding it was too early to get up, Kyria pushed the cats off, rolled on her side and went back to sleep.

Throughout the day Kyria tried to do small household chores. Put dishes in the dishwasher, make the bed, put towels in the washer and then the drier. Each became more difficult than the one before. She ordered a pizza delivery. It could be both lunch and supper. That and pain medicine.

Tuesday, the litter needed done again. Chinese was delivered, a small amount eaten with more of the pain med. The containers were left on the coffee table on top of the pizza box.

Mexican was Wednesday's lunch and supper, but much less was eaten compared to the narcotic she took for the pain. She simply hurt all over. Now she couldn't remember when she'd taken the last dose of meds. Another one couldn't hurt and maybe she'd get a little relief. Maybe she'd sleep. It was getting harder with the pain.

Kyria thought about her comfortable bed, but it was so far away from where she lay on the sofa. A half empty glass of melted ice diluted soda sat beside the bottle of pills. She took one. Cece snuggled between her legs with Mini on the sofa's back looking down at her. Closing her eyes she dosed.

Ufff. Mini landed on Kyria's chest sending throbbing pains through her torso before the cat landed on the floor. It was the cat's subtle way of saying it was suppertime. Kyria got up, went to the bathroom, then fed the cats. Her head felt funny. Sort of fuzzy. When had she taken that last pill? Surely it had been at least four hours ago.

Plopping down on the sofa she reached for the pill bottle. Popping the pill into her mouth she swallowed it with the last drops of soda. Her mouth felt dry. Kyria got up, stumbled into the kitchen and filled the glass with ice and water.

Once again seated on the sofa, she looked at the bottle. Had she taken one? Kyria couldn't remember. She'd gotten a glass of water. It must have been to take a pill. She hurt enough it must have been a long time since she had one. Opening the bottle she shook one into her hand. At least it looked like one. It didn't seem to stop rolling out of the bottle.

Lifting her hand and with a quick motion threw the pill into her mouth. There must be flies in here. They bumped into her face. Where was the water? Concentrating after missing the glass twice, she grasped it and brought it to her mouth. Why did the pill seem so much bigger this time? Oh well.

Kyria lay down and pulled the quilt up. Why was her top wet? She really should get up and change it. Mini snuggled on the pillow next to her head and purred. Such a wonderful sound, purring. So soothing. Why was she thinking of getting up when she was so comfortable with Mini by her head and Cece curled up behind her knees?

CHAPTER SIX

Why didn't Kyria answer the phone? He'd tried all morning. If the aid hadn't come until the afternoon she still should have answered and the aide should have been there by now. Mark looked at his watch; one-thirty. He was off now and could go check on her. Punching the down button he waited impatiently for the elevator.

When Mark arrived at Kyria's building he went straight to the doorman's desk. "I'm Dr. Jenner. Did Ms. Kyria Metcalf leave my name as a possible visitor?"

"Yes sir," Ben said pointing to the elevator.

"Is she there, do you know? I've been trying to reach her by phone and not gotten her?"

"I haven't seen her today and I've been here since six."

"Has her respite aide come today?"

"I haven't seen one come all week. I wasn't here on the weekend but no one has come this week."

Now Mark was worried. Kyria had been sent home with strict instructions to have the aide everyday for at least three weeks, then taper off until she was able to resume caring for herself. "Is the building superintendent around? I'd like to have him go with me in case she doesn't answer the door. I'm concerned about her."

"I'll call him." The doorman looked worried, too.

Mark paced until the large black man came through the door behind the desk.

"I'm Steve Baker, the super. You're concerned about Ms.

Metcalf?"

Mark held out his hand. "I'm Dr. Jenner, Ms. Metcalf's doctor. I've been trying to reach her all day. Now your doorman tells me the respite aide hasn't come all week. I'd appreciate it if you'd go up with me and open her apartment if she doesn't answer."

"Has she gone out, Pete?" Steve asked the doorman.

"No, sir. I haven't seen her this week. She's had some food delivered, but she's not come down."

Mark nearly started tapping his foot, impatient for the man to decide. Something had to be wrong for Kyria not to answer and the aid not to come. He'd let the agency have it if they'd messed up and canceled her care.

"Let's go." Steve turned and led the way to the elevator. "Ms. Metcalf is such a nice tenant. Never gives any trouble. I took care of her cats while she was in the hospital. Funny one, that Mini. Such short legs."

Mark didn't say anything. He was praying. Watching without really seeing Steve press the floor button, Mark simply kept silently praying that she would be all right.

When they got to her apartment Steve knocked on the door. No sound came from inside. "Ms. Metcalf? Kyria? Can you hear me?" Nothing. He looked at Mark then pulled his master key and opened the door.

Mark pushed in as Steve stepped back. Two grey tabby cats, one with very short legs jumped from the sofa and made a bee-line to Steve. Mark hurried over to the sofa. Kyria lay with her eyes closed, mouth agape and right arm hanging down to the floor. Kneeling, he placed figures to her wrist relieved to feel a strong pulse. "She's alive."

"Thank God." Steve's voice came from what Mark thought must be the kitchen as he heard a can crack open as the man pulled the tab.

Mark whipped his stethoscope from his pocket and began examining her. Shallow breathing but a steady, pulse strong. He lifted an eyelid. Kyria jerked and opened her eyes.

"No. I don't need to be in the hospital. I went home. I'm better." The words were slurred but understandable.

"You are home. Just lie quietly while I look you over." Kyria obeyed, closing her eyes.

Mark stood and looked around. A box with a pizza was on the coffee table with only two slices eaten. Several Chinese food containers and other takeout boxes along with empty glasses and soda cans shared the space. None of the containers had more than a few bites missing. A prescription pill bottle was lying on its side with the top and a few pills scattered nearby. On the floor were several more pills. He picked up the bottle. It was the pain medicine he'd ordered when she left the hospital. He knelt beside her again.

"Kyria," he said. "Kyria, how many did you take and when?" She didn't answer. "Kyria, Kyria. Wake up. How many and when did you take them?" Mark tapped her cheeks.

"Take what?" Her words were slurred.

"Your pain meds."

"When I got a drink of water." Kyria tried to roll onto her side away from him.

"Do you need an ambulance?" Steve asked from behind him.

"Let's see if she can walk. It might be that she just took a couple too close together. I'd rather not take her to the hospital. She'd be classified as a drug overdose and that would follow her the rest of her life."

"Okay."

"Help me get her up."

The men gently helped her to stand, Mark cautioning Steve about her injuries. They were glad she was wearing a t-shirt and boxer shorts. Kyria protested that she wanted to sleep. They walked her around the living room a couple of times. She leaned heavily on them. Then she stopped and stood up straight.

"I need to excuse myself for a few minutes. I'll be right back." Kyria stepped away and proceeded to collapse when her legs buckled.

"She needs to…" Steve looked at Mark. "You're the doc. You get to help her."

"Um, the nurses take care of this, not the doctors."

"You're closer to a nurse than I am. I just take care of people's pets when they can't."

"Okay, but help me get her to the bathroom, will you?"

Steve beat a hasty retreat once they had her standing in the bathroom. Mark, very uncomfortable, helped her with the boxers and onto the stool. He left in a hurry telling her to call when she was finished. The men stood outside the closed door in an awkward silence.

They heard a flush then water running. Mark opened the door and peeked in. He could feel his face heating up. Leaning over the sink, her head against the mirror, Kyria was washing her hands. The boxers were on the floor and the t-shirt barely covered her bottom.

"Um, Kyria, do you need any help?" Mark pulled his head back hoping she could put the boxers on by herself.

"I can't get my pants. Can you help?" Each word was slurred into the next.

Steve shot Mark a look of amusement. "I never thought I'd be glad I wasn't smart enough to be a doctor."

"Thanks." Mark went into the bathroom keeping his eyes away from Kyria's body. Snatching up the boxers he held them up to her. She lifted a foot and held it out toward him. Swallowing, he slipped the Tweetie Bird boxers onto the foot. Kyria put that one down nearly pulling Mark over since he was holding the shorts at arm's length. She lifted the other foot. He slipped the boxers over it and when her foot was again on the floor he stood and exited saying, "You can do the rest. I'll come back in a moment."

"Man, is your face red," Steve said when Mark was in the hall leaning his forehead against the wall.

"I'll bet. How embarrassing. I'm embarrassed now and she will be if she remembers this. Her boxers had come totally off. The t-shirt covered the essentials, but just barely."

The sound of her collapsing brought them into the bathroom. Picking her up between them they managed to get her from the bathroom and at Mark's direction into the bedroom. Between them they managed to pull the covers away, lay her down, then as she snuggled into her pillow, tucked her in.

"She's not in any danger, so I think it might be best if she sleeps it off."

Steve looked at Kyria, Mark and then at the bedroom door.

"Um, I need to get back to work. Here's my card," he said pulling it from his shirt pocket. "It has my number on it. Call if you need me."

"All right, thanks for the help."

"You're welcome. Ms. Metcalf is a model tenant. I hate to see her like this. Oh, that one's Mini and the other is Cece," Steve said pointing to the grey tabby cats who had jumped onto the bed and were snuggling close to Kyria. "I can let myself out."

Alone now with the sleeping Kyria, Mark looked around the room. It was beautifully decorated with pale yellow walls, lilac and blue fabrics and accents. On the table beside her bed was a Bible with several church bulletins under it. They were from the same church he attended. He'd never seen her there which didn't really surprise him as there were two Sunday morning services, a Sunday night, as well as a number of Bible studies and other events during the week.

Mark hadn't seen any of the pastors visit Kyria in the hospital, but that too wasn't surprising. He wasn't always even on the same floor as her hospital room. He decided to call the church to find out if they even knew she had been in the hospital. There were teams which supplied meals and support for shut-ins, ill and injured members, as well as new additions to a family.

The secretary indicated no one had contacted them about Kyria and they had tried to contact her after she missed a couple of Sundays. They hadn't been able to reach her and no calls had been returned. She thanked him for the information and would pass it on to the pastor.

Mark, having moved to the living room, looked at the mess on the coffee table. Kyria must have spent much of her time on the sofa. The food containers alone attested to that. Several blankets and pillows also gave evidence of it being a spot much used. He went to the kitchen, found a garbage bag and cleaned up the food containers.

Picking up the pill bottle, he counted the remaining pills. Relief that the amount indicated Kyria hadn't been overdosing very much swept through him. Just then the doorbell rang.

Pete, the doorman, stood there when Mark answered the door. "How is Ms. Metcalf?"

"She's sleeping, but will be all right. I think she's simply taken some pain pills too close together. She'll sleep it off and be better tomorrow probably."

"Is there anything I could do for you?"

Mark allowed Pete to take the garbage then was alone again. How to proceed? Leaving Kyria alone wasn't wise. Calling the respite aide company, he frowned when he discovered she had told them other arrangements had been made and she wouldn't be needing their services any longer. Now he knew why she'd been alone with no aide coming to at least check on her.

Mini jumped onto the sofa beside him and crawled onto his lap. Absently, he stroked her softness. He'd need to stay the night to make sure Kyria was all right. Some people became nauseous from regular doses. With however many she'd taken the odds rose.

Now the other cat, what had Steve called her, oh yes, Cece, jumped up beside him bringing Mark out of his revery. The two felines looked at him as if they were asking him questions. Cece reached out a paw patting his arm.

"You two are worried too, aren't you. Kyria will be all right, hopefully tomorrow. I'll stay until she wakes up lucid so I can scold her for getting rid of the respite aide." That reminded him of his schedule. He'd call in saying he needed someone to cover his shift for tomorrow. Mark hadn't a clue about how long Kyria would sleep.

CHAPTER SEVEN

Mark arranged a pillow and blankets on the sofa around ten o'clock getting ready to bed down there for the night. He'd checked on Kyria several times through the evening. Sleeping peacefully, he'd run out to get something to bring back for supper. The cats met him at the door when he returned as if he'd been gone several months.

Moaning coming from Kyria's room took him down the hall. She was sitting on the edge of the bed holding her head.

"How are you feeling?" Mark said softly.

"Go away, Turner. I don't need you. Stop your shirt from changing colors."

Lovely, she was hallucinating. "Kyria, it's Mark Jenner, your doctor from the hospital." He knelt in front of her.

She looked at him then closed her eyes. "I'm not going. I want to stay in Savannah. I want to go to a real school. Why can't we have a cat?"

"You're at home, Kyria. You aren't going anywhere." Why was he trying to talk to her about what was real? The synapses were firing in a nonsensical way. Until enough of the pain medicine metabolized and was flushed from her system her mind wouldn't be able to process correctly.

"I need to pee. Will you please show me to the WC?" The first sentence was spoken in English, the second was fluent French.

"Of course, come with me." Mark helped her rise, noting she was able to stand and walk mostly on her own. He sent up a prayer of gratitude that he wouldn't have to help with her clothing again. He also prayed she wouldn't remember her previous trip.

Hovering in the hall, Mark was encouraged at her steadiness and hoped she would be lucid in the morning. When she opened the door Kyria looked shocked at the sight of him.

"You should have come in a tux to escort me. Those clothes are inappropriate for the event. We'll need to go back to your place so you can change. Mother will make a scene if you arrive like that." Kyria pushed past him and stalked down the hall weaving only slightly.

Mark followed grinning at her indignation. She was in the kitchen trying to open a soda can with a corkscrew. "Here, let me do that for you." He took the can, opened it and handed it back to her.

"Thank you, kind sir. I'm so very thirsty." Kyria lifted the can to her lips and began to drink. Tipping the can too fast, much of the cola ran down her chin onto her t-shirt. Mark nearly groaned. He'd have to get her into a dry one before putting her back to bed. She continued to slug the drink down until the can was empty. Then she set it on the counter and let out a loud unladylike belch.

Mark decided it was time to send her back to bed. "Come, Kyria." He wrapped an arm around her waist guiding her from the kitchen.

She laid her head on his shoulder and sighed. "You're so sweet."

"I know."

Kyria giggled then whispered loudly in his ear. "Can I tell you a secret? I know this doctor who's really cute, but don't tell anyone." She put a finger to her lips and emitted a juicy, "Shush."

Mark pushed her to sit on the edge of the bed. He needed to find another t-shirt or nightshirt. Opening drawers in the bureau he finally located a long purple shirt with glittery hearts and stars all over the front. Now he just needed to get it on her without seeing what he shouldn't.

"Kyria, I need you to stand up."

She popped up like a six year old, swayed a little and smiled.

Leaning close to him she said, "You know that doctor… His name is Jerk Manner. No, Jan Merker. Man Janker? Kann Jerker?"

"Try Mark Jenner." Her confusion filled face nearly caused Mark to laugh out loud. He was more pleased than he'd ever admit that she thought him good looking. "Now turn around." He positioned her facing away from him.

"But you're cute, too. I want to look at you." She spun back around.

"Thank you. You need to be the other way for a couple of minutes though." Mark turned Kyria around again.

"Why?"

"So you can change your shirt. It's wet."

Kyria lifted a hand to her chest. "Oh, it is. Okay." She whipped the shirt over her head and tossed it on the floor. When she started to turn around Mark grabbed her arms.

"Stay still. Here." He pulled the shirt over her head not looking down over her shoulder no matter how much he wanted to. Be a doctor now, man, he scolded himself. He rubbed his forehead as she worked at putting her arms in the sleeves.

"What's happened? My hand isn't where it should be." Kyria turned, thankfully fully covered, but with her hand sticking out of the neck next to her face.

Mark chuckled, reached into the sleeve to grab her wrist and pull her hand out. "Better now?"

"Yeah, thanks." Kyria leaned forward and tried to kiss him on the cheek. Nearly falling over, it landed on his shoulder.

Mark caught her and gently sat her on the bed. "Bedtime, Kyria, snuggle in."

"Okay, Mamie, but I want to stay up late tomorrow." Kyria lay down pulling her pillow into a bunch under her head. Mark tucked the covers around her. Kyria sighed, "Love you."

Mark's heart jumped. "Love you, too." He stood looking at her for a moment before walking to the door and shutting off the light.

~~~~~

Coffee, he needed coffee. Trying to sit up Mark found a cat sitting on his chest looking into his eyes with wide golden ones.

Which one was this? They looked the same to him. It stood up. It didn't look much taller than it had when sitting. Man, what short legs. It must be Mini. He'd never seen a cat like this before.

"You have to move. I need coffee." Mark picked the cat off his chest and sat up, putting Mini on the floor. He grabbed his phone off the table to check the time. Seven-ten. He was glad he'd called for a replacement for his shift today, the night had been difficult.

Mark had slept fitfully checking on Kyria a few times between her nightmares and wanderings. She had cried out several times in obvious terror at something. He'd rushed into her room to find her sitting up staring at whatever was occurring in her dream. Then she'd collapse weeping in his arms when he sat on the bed beside her.

Once, he'd been asleep and she'd plopped down on him thinking she was sitting down on an empty sofa. Her delicate, "pardon me," in what he thought might be Italian had made him grin. Another time he'd been awoken when she was rummaging in the fridge looking for something to eat. When he'd managed to move her away so he could close the door she'd been asleep on her feet.

After he made coffee Mark turned to find both cats blocking the exit to the kitchen. Mini was perched just like a prairie dog. "My you are cute, and apply named. I suppose you two want fed." Cece made her pleasure known by rubbing his legs as he rummaged through cupboards to find the cans of food.

Leaving the cats noisily eating the goo he thought smelled awful, Mark checked on the sleeping Kyria. She was sprawled across the bed, her long hair a tangled mess indicating a restless sleep.

Mark folded the sofa quilt and put the pillow he'd borrowed back on her bed. A cup of coffee helped him clear the cobwebs from his head. Next, he wanted a shower and headed toward the bathroom.

Mark was just starting to button his shirt when the doorbell rang. He thought it was probably Steve coming to check on Kyria so he left it unbuttoned as he hurried to the door. Opening it, he just stared for a moment.

"Oh, good morning, ladies. Come in." It was three ladies from the church each carrying what appeared to be containers of food.

"Dr. Jenner," one said, definitely surprised to see him. "I'm Noreen Alter. Pastor McCachron called and told us Kyria Metcalf had been injured and needed some meals. We've come to deliver them."

"Come in ladies. Kyria is still asleep. I know she'll appreciate the food. It's very kind of you." Mark backed up to allow the ladies into the apartment. Each looked at him with censure. The last looked at his bare chest then into his eyes. Mark nearly groaned. She had been chasing him for several years. Her eyes held disappointment with a dash of anger thrown in.

Following them into the kitchen he quickly buttoned his shirt. Mark couldn't do anything about his bare feet. His shoes and socks were at the other end of the sofa.

"We'll tell Pastor we delivered the meals and that you were here." He thought the speaker this time was the wife of one of the elders. Disapproval was screaming from her voice and body language. What were they so upset about? Relief filled him when they filed past him on their way out the door.

CHAPTER EIGHT

Kyria rolled onto her back with a groan. Her head throbbed causing her to wonder if she'd fallen, hitting it against a battleship. This wasn't the pain she was used to having after the explosion. She even had some nausea. A cool wet cloth was placed across her eyes. Oh, it felt so good. She moaned and placed a hand on her forehead.

"How are you feeling?" It was a male voice… Dr. Jenner's. Kyria opened her eyes beneath the cloth.

"Am I in the hospital?"

"No, you're at home. You took too many pain pills. We'll talk when you feel a little better."

Kyria closed her eyes again. She tried to remember when she had taken the pills but everything was a blur. Pulling the cloth away she said, "I'm going to the bathroom. I'll come to the living room in a few minutes." She hoped he would leave but no sound of his moving away was heard so she opened her eyes to see him standing beside the bed.

"I'll help you. You may be a little unsteady on your feet."

It was obvious any protests that she could manage by herself would be futile so Kyria sat up swinging her legs over the edge of the bed. The room swayed and Mark's hand came to rest gently on her shoulder.

"Easy now, slowly."

Kyria looked at her shirt noticing it was a different one than she remembered having on. Heat shot up her neck and across her cheeks faster than a bullet leaving a gun she thought. Unless there was someone else in her apartment he must have changed her shirt.

"Are you ready to try and stand?" Mark's voice was gentle. Kyria tipped her head back to look at him. Nodding, she took his offered hand and rose to her feet.

"Slowly, I'm sure you have a massive headache. Is your stomach upset?"

They walked through the room heading to the bathroom. "A little. Better than a few minutes ago."

"Good. I'll get some crackers and soda for when you're done."

Closing the bathroom door, Kyria leaned against it. How humiliating. No, she wouldn't think about him changing her shirt. Or any other ways he might have helped with her personal needs.

Her mouth tasted awful. Moving to the sink she looked in the mirror as she fumbled for her toothbrush. Oh my, what a tangled mess. Her thick mass of wavy hair was haloing her face in anything but an attractive manner. Mark would have to wait until she got it under control.

~~~~~

Mark waited with a can of Sprite and sleeve of crackers trying to decide how much to tell her of how he had found her and what all had occurred during the day and night. He knew Kyria would be embarrassed. Maybe just stick to the main points. He'd been worried when he couldn't get a hold of her so he'd come over and had the super open her apartment.

They'd determined she'd taken too many pills too close together and he'd stayed so she'd have someone with her through the night. That was good. Just the bare facts. He looked at his watch. It had been fifteen minutes. How long did it take to go and brush your teeth? He heard the bathroom door open then another door close. She must be changing into different clothes.

~~~~~

Kyria pulled out a pair of pajama pants and long sleeved t-shirt, then a pair of wooly socks, changing as quickly as her dizzy head would allow her. Her stomach told her it was time to sit down so Kyria took a slow deep breath and ventured to the living room.

Mark was seated on the sofa. "Come sit here." He had stood

and was directing her to the opposite end. "Put your feet up. I've got some crackers and Sprite. They should help your stomach."

Kyria sat, sipped and nibbled. She hadn't a clue as to what to say. Ashamed, she just sat. Mark drew her feet into his lap and began rubbing first one, then the other.

"Kyria, why were you alone? Where is the aide?"

"Um... The first aide was so good and sweet. Then her husband and children were ill. The aide they sent on the weekend was... well... not as helpful. I decided not to have her back."

"I see." His disapproval flowed over her.

"I was doing fine."

"I beg to differ with you, Kyria. You overdosed on pain meds and were unconscious when Steve and I found you. Then you were hallucinating. If I hadn't been here you may have left the apartment and who knows what would have happened."

Kyria sat and just looked at her hands fidgeting with the edge of the quilt folded over the back of the sofa. His hands had stilled on her feet.

"You had my phone number. I'd given you my card. If the aide was unsatisfactory you could have called me. Or called the agency. They would have sent a different one."

"I know... It's just..." Not thinking of a good reason why she hadn't, at least one that he would accept, she quit speaking.

Mini jumped onto Kyria then walked up her chest to butt her head on Kyria's chin. She drew the cat close which elicited loud purring. Cece jumped up, looked at Kyria then walked to Mark climbing into his lap to curl up, obviously settling to sleep.

"So what's with the short legs on that one?" Mark asked pointing at Mini.

Kyria was glad he wasn't going to push her into confessing her stupidity. They both knew she'd stubbornly chosen to ignore her need for help. She explained about the new breeds of Munchkin and Minuette cats with the short legs and kitten personality. It was nice to have someone to talk with. Someone who cared enough to stay with her when she was sick. No one had since Mamie.

Shame flooded Kyria. She wasn't sick. She'd overdosed on

pain pills and he'd had to stay to make sure she was all right. It wasn't because he cared for her more than as a patient. Her actions had inconvenienced him. Her stomach started to ache as she thought about all he'd done for her. How could she have done this to such a nice man?

"Ohhhh." Kyria put her hands to her head then lay over with her face buried in the pillow on the arm of the sofa. Her stomach turned. She got up as quickly as she could and hurried to the bathroom making it to the toilet just in time as her stomach rejected the crackers and Sprite.

A warm wet cloth was pressed into her hand when she was finished. It was then she realized someone had been holding her hair back. Kyria wiped her face and mouth then threw the cloth in the direction of the hamper.

"Here, rinse your mouth." Mark's voice was full of compassion. He handed her a glass of cool water.

Kyria obeyed the command then slumped against the wall looking up at Mark standing close by. He closed the lid of the stool, flushed and picked her up, taking her to her bedroom and proceeded to tuck her in.

"You sleep a while. We'll see if you can keep something down later."

"I'll be fine. You must need to get to the hospital." Kyria felt simply awful both physically and emotionally.

"I don't need to go in today. I called a friend to cover for me. I'll be here when you wake up."

Kyria turned away from him and pulled the blankets over her shoulders. She didn't want him to see her tears. She'd brought this on both of them. Her pride and desire to rely on herself. The disapproval of the weekend aide had pricked memories. Now she'd caused so much trouble for Mark. Her sin had rippled over, affecting a man who had only looked out for her welfare. She would do whatever was necessary to make things right for Mark.

CHAPTER NINE

The darkness of the room when Kyria awoke told her it was at least evening if not night. The bedside clock said 8:12 so somewhere in between. She took a deep breath and stretched. Her stomach growled. Maybe she'd be able to eat a little something. Her head felt better, too. The body aches she'd had since the explosion were there. Kyria wondered where her pain pills were, then remembered. She rubbed a shaky hand over her face.

"Please, Lord, make this all go away. I'm so ashamed. Help me figure out what to do. How to make up for this whole thing." Kyria wanted to roll over and simply hide forever. Nature's call made her get out of bed.

The bedroom door opened then the bathroom one shut alerting Mark that Kyria was awake. Soon she would come out, he hoped, and join him in the living room. He'd eaten some of a chicken casserole one of the ladies from church had brought. Mark made a plate for Kyria ready to pop into the microwave when she got up, hoping she could eat and keep the food down. He'd gotten a can of Sprite out of the fridge and the sleeve of crackers to test her stomach before the casserole.

Mark had spent the afternoon thinking about her. Kyria's job was waiting for her. The HR guy had told him she was a talented interior designer. Her apartment was beautifully decorated. The items weren't high-end or expensive. Everything was also well kept.

She probably didn't have a lot of money since the apartment

was small and he knew the neighborhood wasn't a prime one. He liked this decorating better than his. It was a little small for his taste but adequate.

Looking up when he heard her coming toward him Mark saw Kyria had changed into sweatpants and a sweatshirt. Her hair was confined in a loose braid hanging over her shoulder. It was how she'd kept it while she was in the hospital after they'd brought her out of the drug induced coma.

"How are you feeling?" Mark asked.

"A bit better. My stomach is growling which hopefully says I can eat now."

"It's a good sign. Here, try these again." He handed her the Sprite and crackers as she sat down beside him on the sofa. "If you can keep them down there's some pretty good chicken casserole. I made you a plate."

"Thanks." Kyria nibbled a cracker looking vaguely out the windows. The lights of buildings sprinkling them like stars.

"Um, I fed the cats."

She grinned a little. "They let you know they were hungry, I'll bet."

Mark chuckled. "Most definitely." He watched as she took a sip of soda. Her forehead furrowed. Kyria turned her face to him, eyes filled with sorrow.

"I'm so sorry to have inconvenienced you. I'll try not to bother you again. Why didn't you just take me to the hospital? You could have just gotten me there and headed home. I would have been taken care of."

Something in him tightened at the thought of Kyria exiting his life.

"You would have been classified as a drug overdose and the police would have had to be contacted. It would have followed you the rest of your life. I didn't want that to happen." Mark realized he might have been able to forestall any reporting since he was one of her doctors. He'd wanted to tend to her himself and couldn't if she was in the hospital.

"Thank you... I think." Her brow furrowed more. "What now?"

"I'm not sure." They sat silently for a while, then Mark asked,

"How's your stomach handling the crackers?"

"It seems fine. Think it would handle some casserole?"

"Probably." Mark went to the kitchen with Kyria trailing behind. She got out a fork and sat on a counter stool while he warmed the plate in the microwave.

He watched her as she ate. Her comment about him leaving her at the hospital and going home didn't sit well with him. Even if he had taken her to the hospital he would have stayed with her. But then, he'd never even thought to stay after hours with any other patient.

"How's the food settling?"

"Seems fine. Dr. Jenner, I'm afraid to take the pain meds, but I hurt."

"That's understandable. Ibuprofen will at least take the edge off. The pain should lessen a little more each day. Try taking 800 milligrams. I'll write out a script for you. Oh, I called the respite aide agency. They'll be sending Amisa tomorrow."

"But..."

"No buts. You will have an aide. I also requested you not have the same weekend one as before, which is what you should have done. They have enough so you didn't have to be alone." Mark gave her a stern look pulling his eyebrows together.

~~~~~

Kyria was pouring milk into a glass the next morning when the doorbell rang. Amisa stood holding her big orange bag with a frown on her face.

"If you were one of my children I'd turn you over my knee and spank you good. Telling the agency you'd made other arrangements and wouldn't need an aide." Amisa brushed past Kyria coming into the apartment. "What were you thinking?"

"I know. Stupid decision, but that aide they sent over the weekend was simply awful. She wasn't friendly, hardly did anything and disapproved of my cats." Kyria unsuccessfully kept tears from filling her eyes as she closed the door.

"Aw baby, come here and let me give you a hug." Amisa dropped her purse and wrapped her arms around Kyria. "You learned the hard way, didn't you. Some of us have to do most things the hard way instead of the easy way."

"You sound like Mamie. She was my nanny as I grew up. I loved her more than…" Kyria stopped before she revealed too much. "Thank you for the scolding." She grinned sheepishly.

"Well, if you pull any more boneheaded stunts like that I will give you more than a scolding, you can be sure. Come, let's get the vitals done then you can tell me all about it."

By the time Amisa left Kyria felt much better. Amisa had teased her from her guilt and helped her wash her hair. The thickness and length when wet was more than Kyria could manage in her weakened condition.

~~~~~

Kyria decided she needed to call the head of the Children's Church team and let her know why she'd missed so many weeks and wouldn't be able to help for who knows how long.

"Hello," Mrs. Beckel said when she answered Kyria's call.

"Hello, this is Kyria Metcalf. I'm calling to let you know why I haven't been showing up for my times working in Children's Church." Kyria went on to explain about the explosion and her hospitalization. She knew she wouldn't be able to handle the job for a while longer.

"That's fine. I was going to contact you anyway. We won't be able to have you work with the children anymore. We can't have people of questionable morals influencing them."

"Pardon me?"

"I'm sure you know what I'm talking about so I won't elaborate. Just know you are off the team. Have a good day." Mrs. Beckel hung up leaving Kyria with her mouth hanging open in shock.

What was the woman talking about? Questionable moral character? Kyria had liked working with the children and other adults on the team. Pastor MacCachron encouraged her to get involved and work on becoming friends with some others in church. She'd tried. It had been difficult, but she'd started to enjoy it. Now this. For some reason Mrs. Beckel found her unworthy to continue. Would she ever be able to feel accepted and worthy? Was she so incompetent that she couldn't even help someone tend children?

Oh no! Her overdosing on the pain medication. The ladies

who brought the casseroles, they must have told Mrs. Beckel. She must think I'm a druggy.

Discouraged, Kyria lay down on her bed, tears slipping over her eyelids, curled up in a ball and asked, again, for God to forgive her for taking all those pills.

~~~~~

Giggles and whispers seemed to follow Mark around the hospital. On each floor conversations stopped when he arrived at the nurses' stations all morning. It had happened when he'd first been hired but as the time progressed the attention to the single good-looking doctor had faded. Now only when a new employee was hired did he receive longing looks and suggestive comments. There was nothing he could do about it, whatever it was they were giggling about, so he chose to ignore them and do his work.

Mark also thought about Kyria, a lot. He wanted to call her to see how she was doing but hadn't done so yet. Instead he'd called the agency and gotten the aide's report for over the weekend. Maybe he'd call when he got off work.

Instead, he worked a double and went home exhausted, going straight to bed since he had surgery the next morning.

CHAPTER TEN

"Hey, you sly dog, you."

Mark looked at Keith Austin, surgeon, in confusion. He was sitting in the locker room changing into scrubs. He was assisting in surgery today, keeping his skills and accreditation up.

"What?"

"Here I thought you were pure and lily white where women are concerned. Now I hear you spent the night with a former patient." Keith laughed and punched Mark in the arm.

"What?"

"You know, that girl who was the explosion victim. You treated her while she was here. I heard you spent the night with her."

"It's not like that. She'd OD'ed on pain pills and was hallucinating. I just made sure she was okay." Mark wondered how Keith knew.

"Yeah, right. Good cover story." The surgeon chuckled as he pulled on the light green pants.

Mark gritted his teeth. It wouldn't do any good to say any more. Keith had made up his mind and defending himself would only make him look guiltier.

"So," Keith leaned close. "Was she good?"

"That's enough." Now Mark was angry. He'd take the comments about himself, but when Kyria was insulted he drew the line.

"Okay, okay. I get it. Change of subject. Let's go over the case while we scrub."

Still wearing the surgical garb, Mark was standing at a nurses station later studying a patient chart when arms wrapped around his waist and a body pressed close to his back. Startled, he jumped trying to move away.

"Hi, Sugar. Just letting you know I'm available now that you've broken out of the good boy act." The voice was a nurse's who had been chasing him ever since he'd started working there.

"Not interested, Julie. I've told you before," Mark said as he pulled her arms apart and stepped away turning to face her.

"Don't kid me. That little bomb victim can't hold a candle to me." Julie moved in again, this time pressing herself to Mark's front. When he opened his mouth to speak she swooped in, mashed her mouth to his and stuck her tongue in.

Mark shoved her away, disgusted at her boldness. It was all he could do not to wipe his mouth right in front of her. "Leave me alone. What you're doing now makes me doubly, no triply, sure I'll never be interested." He stalked away heading to the men's room where he not only wiped but rinsed his mouth out.

Frustration had him leaning against the wall thinking. Who had told someone at the hospital? He knew Keith and Julie weren't believers, not even close, but someone who claimed to be had brought the news to the hospital.

What am I going to do, Lord? He'd thought maybe the ladies who brought the food would keep it to themselves. Who else could it be? It must have been one or more of the ladies who'd spread the tale. Both his good name and Kyria's were being slandered and nothing could be done about it.

"Dr. Jenner." Mark looked around as he exited the restroom. Nurse Gadsden was approaching and she didn't look happy.

"Can I help you with something?"

"No, I just want to tell you how disappointed I am in you. Here I thought you were one of the good Christians who actually live what the Bible says."

Mark stood stunned, trying to understand.

"How could you lead that poor girl on like that, then use her in such a nasty way? And with no parents or family or friends. She trusted and looked up to you. I respected you and to think you used to be one of my favorite doctors. I'm ashamed of you." Nurse Gadsden turned on her heal and stomped away.

Mark watched her walk away sure now that everyone thought he'd done more than sleep on Kyria's sofa. He hated that he was thought to be a cad, but the slight to Kyria's reputation turned his stomach. What could he do to make it right?

He walked down the hall to the doctor's lounge. Keith and another man who Mark knew slept around were drinking coffee. The other doctor lifted his cup in silent salute when Mark entered. Disgusted, he poured himself a cup and left making his way to the tranquility garden. It was empty so he sat on a bench.

The area was fenced in with a spillway fountain pouring from a rock wall into a small pond. There weren't any flowers blooming this early in the spring but the buds on the trees were swelling and turning from gray to pale green or red. In a few weeks daffodils and tulips would fill the space with a riot of color. Even now green shoots poked up from the different flower beds.

"What are we going to do?" He asked the question out loud. He really was attracted to her. He wanted to date her but wondered if it would fuel the rumors at church and here at the hospital. Would that make it better or worse? Should he tell her about the rumors or keep the gossip about them to himself?

There was some verse about living properly among the ungodly and even if they accuse you of doing something wrong, by continuing to live right they'll honor God at the last days. Didn't really help now but it was a promise to keep doing right. But what was right? Did he abandon his attraction to Kyria just because some gossiping, self-righteous women spread stories they didn't know the details of?

Mark spent some time in prayer asking for guidance. He wanted to pursue a relationship with her. There was gossip being spread from members of the church they both went to. Another verse came to mind. It was from James. It was about people who profess to be religious but don't keep a tight rein on their tongues. Their religion is worthless. Yeah, he thought. It's what gives Christians a bad name. Flapping their jaws with lies and innuendo. Of course, they do it with the best intentions. They'll pray for the poor sinner as they spread whatever they think was the truth.

So, what to do? Mark spent some more time asking for

guidance. He didn't want to hurt Kyria. It seemed that either way, pursue a relationship and fuel the gossips or cheat himself, and her, of a potential lifetime of happiness.

Remembering the verses of the devotion he'd read that morning, Mark pulled out his smartphone. He wanted to read them again. Opening the app he found it. Proverbs 3:5-6: *Trust in the Lord with all your heart and lean not on your own understanding; in all your ways submit to him, and he will make your paths straight.*

There was his answer. He needed to trust with all his heart. He didn't need to figure it all out. The Lord would make the path straight. With a deep breath, he released the tension that had tightened his shoulders and back. It was in God's hands. Standing, he shoved is phone into his pocket and headed back into the hospital.

Mark ended his shift several hours later. He was disgusted with the staff. At least, some of them. The news of his night at Kyria's had traveled faster than the speed of light, in his opinion. A few let him know they understood the situation and knew he was innocent. Others teased him about his fall from celibacy. More than one woman let him know they were available, whenever and wherever. The lack of character astounded him. He thought medical professionals would hold to a higher moral standard, at least at work.

He changed back into street clothes and went to his car, mulling the entire situation over. The peace he'd found in the tranquility garden abandoned him.

Mark decided to call his brother-in-law, a good friend and minister. Charles (Hutch) Hutchinson had grown up a few doors down from the Jenner household. He and Mark had been close friends. The bond had tightened when Hutch married Mark's younger sister Chloe. Now he looked forward to the birth of his sister's first child. Hutch would help him sort this all out.

CHAPTER ELEVEN

"So that's the whole story, Hutch. What do you think?" Mark was lying on his bed staring at the ceiling while speaking with his brother-in-law on the phone. "I'm trying to discern what the Holy Spirit is telling me but I can't seem to come to a conclusion."

"How come you never ask me the easy questions? Why do you always come to me with the hard and off beat ones?"

"My pastor can answer the easy ones. I save up the good ones for you."

"Gee thanks." Hutch was silent for a few moments. "It can be very difficult to figure out if it's the Holy Spirit telling you something. First Thessalonians five nineteen through twenty-one says to not stifle the Holy Spirit or despise prophecy but test everything holding on to what's good and staying away from all evil."

"So how do I do that?" Mark grabbed a tennis ball off the bedside table and began to throw it toward the ceiling and catching it with his free hand.

"The Holy Spirit would never instruct you to do something sinful. To go against the commands of God."

"Well, dating isn't against it. Neither is marriage, if it were to progress that far."

"Is this woman, what's her name again?"

"Kyria."

"Is she a believer? If she's not I don't think God would encourage you to date her."

"Yes, she goes to the same church as I do. I didn't know that until the other night. We'd talked about our faith while she was in the hospital and prayed together several times.

"You know, Hutch, Kyria doesn't seem to have anyone. There's a man who she calls Uncle Russ who isn't really her uncle. Her parents are deceased. I think she has a brother, but he's not in evidence."

"Be careful you don't look at her as a damsel in distress."

"Yeah, it would be easy to. I feel protective of her. I had planned to continue some sort of relationship with her. I'm drawn to her."

"Well, that's a positive anyway. So you're attracted to her?"

"Yeah, it's a little hard to think of at this point since she's still healing. The other night and morning she wasn't at her best, but at least I know how she'd look in the morning." Mark chuckled as did Hutch.

"So what kind of message do you think you're supposed to get here? Has our discussion given you any answers or thoughts?"

"Well, I'm not ready to propose to her, but I'm thinking it could be a possibility. I'm pretty attracted to her."

"What about falling in love?"

"Kyria is the only woman since high school I've even thought about a second time. So, yeah. I might, but if I don't date her how can I know? If dating her makes the gossips keep talking and causes her hurt— Man, the thought just makes me so angry. She's done nothing to deserve this sort of thing."

They were both silent for several moments.

"Mark, the best thing you can do at the moment is pray. Also, search for verses on guidance. Here's another verse for you. Proverbs 31:10 *An excellent wife who can find? She is far more precious than jewels.* Just remember God has plans for your good. He has them for Kyria, too. There's no hurry. Don't you be in one.

"If you decide to date her that's all well and good since she's a believer. Marriage is for a lifetime. It's a covenant between three, you, her and God. Don't mistake wanting to be a knight in armor rescuing a damsel in distress for a real Christ centered relationship."

"I won't. Thanks for the advice. I appreciate being able to lay it all out to someone not involved."

"Now wait a minute. I'm married to your sister. That makes me involved. She'd make me sleep on the sofa if my advice led you to do something stupid."

Mark laughed. "Chloe would do that, too. I'm her favorite brother."

"At least today," Hutch shot back with a chuckle. "Keep me posted. If you suddenly announce an engagement, I want to be warned. Your folks may have heart attacks. Their only unmarried, career driven son succumbing to a woman."

"I know, I know. Now let me hang up. I need to talk with Kyria. Thanks again." Mark hung up continuing to lie on the bed. Lord, help me know what it is you want me to do. Us to do. I never thought about getting married much. I've been too busy getting established. Now though, Mark found the idea not too bad. Sure he wasn't 'in love' with Kyria. At least not yet, but he liked her. He'd paid her more attention than any other patient. He'd never wanted to keep in contact with any before.

Mark got off the bed deciding to take a shower then go over to see Kyria. Maybe he'd grab something at the grocery so they could fix supper. Grabbing his cell phone, he punched her number. He'd have to program it in if they were going to have a relationship.

"Hello?"

"Hi Kyria, it's Mark Jenner. Can I come over so we can talk? I'll bring the makings for supper."

"I don't know, can you?" Her voice held a teasing note.

"Huh?"

"My tutor used to say that when I used 'can' incorrectly. Can infers the ability. Yes, you may come over." She stressed the word 'may' then laughed. "I only mention that to people I like, so feel privileged."

"Oh, I do." Mark laughed, too. "What would you like me to get at the market?"

"Shrimp. I don't care what else, but I want shrimp."

"What's the magic word?" Mark grinned as he teased her back.

"Please sir, I want some shrimp."

"You got it, babe. I'll see you in about an hour."

~~~~~

Kyria closed her phone. He'd called her babe and was coming in an hour. Suddenly, she panicked. An hour. All she had was an hour to get ready. She hurried to the bedroom pulling the sweatshirt off as she went. All Mark had seen her in were hospital gowns, t-shirts, sweats and boxers. She wanted him to see her looking, well, at least presentable.

Looking in her closet, Kyria struggled to choose something flattering yet what she would wear at home. This wasn't a date. He was coming to talk about the situation and make dinner nothing more. She finally decided on a red sweater and jeans. Pinning her hair on top of her head she took a shower letting the warm water sooth the aches away. After her shower, she felt fresh and knew she looked better than when Mark had seen her last.

Kyria was stunned when she pulled on her jeans. They were way too big. She looked at herself carefully in the mirror. She hadn't realized she had lost so much weight. Her cheeks were gaunt, her stomach almost sunken. Kyria had never been fat but had carried a few extra pounds. Now she nearly looked anorexic. No wonder the nursing staff had been urging her to eat more.

Pulling the sweater over her head Kyria frowned. It hung like a tent. At least she hadn't shrunk too much up top. Those curves were still there.

Well, scratch the jeans, she'd have to shop for new ones. Digging in her chest of drawers she found a pair of blue yoga pants. They hadn't quite fit before but, boy oh boy, did they fit now. She smiled. Adding a gold belt over her sweater fancied her outfit up somewhat but with a stay at home feel. It also highlighted her now very narrow waist and hips along with her shapely bust. Kyria was pleased with how she looked.

Just as she slipped on some comfortable shoes the doorbell rang. Rats, she didn't have time for any makeup or jewelry. Kyria glanced at her phone. Early, he was early. No wonder she didn't have time. Well, he'd seen her looking worse. At least her hair was having a good day. That was always a plus. It fell in deep waves across her shoulders and down her back. She pinched her cheeks and bit her lips as she went to answer the door.

"Hi, Dr. Jenner." Kyria refrained from telling him he was early as she held the door so he could maneuver in with the grocery bags to the counter. He was dressed in a gray t-shirt and blue jeans. She'd never seen him this casual.

"Hi, first you need to start calling me by my first name. It's Mark." His grin denied any sting in his words. "I got shrimp, potatoes, peas, salad mixings and, ta dah." Mark pulled a deli tray with a dozen chocolate chocolate chip cookies from a bag. "They just put these out. Baked not over an hour ago. Thought they'd be good for dessert.

"Yummy." Kyria used a fingernail to break through the plastic wrap, pulled one out and took a bite. "Oh, so good."

"Hey, those are for later, after the meal." Mark grabbed it from her.

"Ah, come on. I haven't had anything good like this is so long. Besides, I just saw what I really look like and I can use those calories." She stomped her foot in mock frustration, trying to reach for the cookie he held high above her head.

Mark looked her over, still holding the cookie away from her. She felt his eyes scan her face then down her body. Kyria felt herself blush as she wondered what he was thinking.

"Oh all right, but I get a bite, too." He brought the cookie to his mouth and bit right beside where she had bitten. Something turned over in Kyria chest. She felt another blush coming so she grabbed the cookie, popped what was left in her mouth and began unloading the grocery bags.

"What's this? Wine?" Kyria asked.

"Yes, since you aren't taking the narcotic anymore I thought a glass of wine would be nice. Chateau la box white zinfandel, a very good year, too."

Kyria laughed and handed the box to him. "Okay, you be the sommelier and pull the cork, er, spigot out. I'll get a couple of glasses."

"Wow, fancy word." Mark chuckled.

"Yeah, it means wine guy. Well, technically wine steward, but wine guy works." Kyria handed him the glasses.

Mark filled each one about half full, handing one to her. "To your return to health, work and the future." He looked at Kyria as they clinked the glasses together then sipped. Even as thin as she was, he'd noticed when she'd mentioned it, he thought she was lovely. High cheekbones, green eyes sparkling, lips pursed to sip from the glass. And her hair. It seemed to be several colors at once; light brown shading to blonde. This was the first time he'd seen it brushed out loose down her back. His fingers itched to feel its softness.

Lord, you have given me an attraction for her, I'll give you that. If you're telling me to get serious with her then you have to be the one to do the convincing. Mark watched silently while Kyria put the food in the fridge. It was too early to start supper. Nothing they had would take long to fix.

"Come, let's sit down and talk." Mark took her hand leading Kyria to the sofa. He arranged her so she was reclining, then sat at the other end. He wanted to massage her feet again but decided not touching her would be better for now. Actually, he wanted to run his hands up and down her calves, but pushed that thought away.

"Kyria, I'd like to continue seeing you in a nonprofessional capacity." *Boy, what a romantic way of putting it. I need to sweeten this up.* "I mean I'd like to date you. I've been attracted to you since you woke from the coma. I had to keep our relationship professional before, but now I'd like to get to know you, not as your doctor." Mark looked at Kyria's face. Her mouth was open in shock.

"You want to date me? Me? Why?"

Mark put a hand on her foot. "Because I like you. You're sweet and funny. Smart and nice. And I want to run my hands through your hair to see how soft it is." *Why did he say that? Couldn't he control his mouth?* The verses in James of controlling the tongue flitted through his mind. He noticed his hand had slid around to her calf and pulled it away.

"I...I...I, yes, I'd like to go out with you," Kyria's stuttering caused Mark to wonder.

"You sure? You don't sound very enthusiastic."

Kyria swung her feet to the floor, sat up and leaned close to him. She smiled. "Yes, I like you, too, and would love to get to know you in a purely nonprofessional way."

Mark took that as a hint and ran a hand through her hair to behind her neck, pulling her face to his and kissed her softly.

CHAPTER TWELVE

Oh my. He tasted good. Much better than Reginald Brubaker had when he'd kissed her at a New Year's party she'd gone to with her parents years ago. The fact that Reginald had been covered with zits and had bad breath might have something to do with it, but Kyria didn't think so. Her stomach was doing a funny dance, too, which was vastly different from the turning it had done when Reginald kissed her.

"You taste good." Mark still had his hand on her neck holding her close. "Come sit closer."

Kyria felt shy but did as he asked. Mark pulled her against him settling her back to his chest and wrapping his arm around her shoulders.

"So, how did your day go? Any interesting sick people?"

Mark laughed. "No. I assisted with surgery. The rest was pretty ordinary." Kyria noticed a flatness to his voice. Maybe a difficulty with a patient. "How about you? Did Amisa come?"

"Yes, and I got a scolding and the threat of a spanking if I did something like that again."

"Just as you should. I'll spank you, too, if you do something like that again." Mark tightened his arm around her for a moment lending emphasis to his words.

Kyria thought about Mrs. Beckel and that she had been removed from her church work. She decided not to mention it. Mark didn't need to know about the fallout from her mistake.

They spent the time before they fixed supper chatting, then worked together making their meal. Kyria was careful to take every direction Mark gave her in preparation. She didn't want to mess this up before it even started.

Mark allowed her one glass of wine with dinner. Kyria noted that he only had two. They laughed about the vintage of the box again as they put the dishes in the dishwasher.

"Come here," Mark said, settling again on the sofa in the same cuddly position. Kyria relaxed against him as he ran his fingers through her hair.

It felt so nice. She hadn't been held in such a way since... Since Mamie had held her when she came for the funeral of her parents. Kyria leaned her head back against Mark's shoulder and sighed. She could sit like this forever.

Mark gently twirled his finger in her hair. It was softer than he'd expected. He wondered how it kept its wave, being so soft. Chloe had groused often about how straight her hair became when it was long; the weight pulling all the curl out. She kept it short for that reason.

Kyria's hair was full of wave and bounce. The nurses had commented on how it got in the way so they'd tied it back. Mark thought of the braid Kyria had them put it into when she came out of the coma. Maybe that was how it got so many waves.

Hearing her sigh as Kyria leaned her head back felt wonderful. Mark adjusted so she would be more comfortable. They were simply sitting quietly enjoying the silence. She felt so good against him. It seemed almost as if something was now complete. He wondered if it was God's way of telling him the relationship was supposed to be.

Lord, you seem to be leading me this way. I've gotten no red flags waved telling me to stop. We'll get to know each other for a while but this feels so right. Slam this door if it's not of you. I don't want to hurt Kyria or me if this isn't of you.

"Kyria, I think it's time for me to leave."

"It's not late."

"No, but I need to leave before I press us farther along in this relationship than I think we're ready for."

Kyria sat up and moved away from him. Mark stood up and held out a hand to her. She allowed him to pull her to standing and they moved hand in hand to the door.

Looking up at him, Kyria hoped he would kiss her again. She really wanted him to kiss her. He'd tasted so good. When he framed her face with his hands she sighed in relief. As his mouth captured the sigh she wrapped her arms around his neck and released herself to his care.

~~~~~

Saturday, Mark told Kyria to dress up since he was taking her out to a nice restaurant. When she opened the door he smiled. Heavens, she was beautiful, still too thin but lovely nonetheless.

"Come here, beautiful, and let me kiss you," he said. Instead she pulled him into her apartment and shut the door.

"We don't need an audience," she said stepping into his arms.

Mark took the hint and kissed her. He marveled at how right she felt in his arms. Lifting his head he set her away from him. "Let me look at you."

Kyria had on a dress of teal and blue swirls which flowed wide to the hem. She twirled and the full sweep spread out as if she were dancing a waltz. The scoop neck and top of the sheer sleeves were covered by a soft yellow shawl. Yellow bead earrings winked from behind her hair which was softly pulled into a knot at the nape of her neck. A matching yellow pendant hung from an omega chain.

"Wow. You do clean up well." Mark pulled out his phone and took her picture then brought her back into his arms. Kyria was smiling. He kissed her again. He loved her smile. "Let's go and show you off."

"I'm glad you like this. It's not new by any means but I've always loved this dress. It makes me feel very feminine."

"Oh honey, you are most definitely feminine."

When they arrived at the restaurant their table wasn't ready so they went to one of the tall tables in the bar. Mark could see other men looking at Kyria with appreciation.

He didn't know how to feel. That this lovely woman was with him pleased him immensely. She held herself with poise and grace. He was proud to have her on his arm. However, the desire on the faces of the men looking at her bothered him beyond belief. Pride and anger fought for dominance within him. Boy, was he proud Kyria was with him. Also, anger that the men were drooling so obviously at her.

Mark helped Kyria onto the tall chair as a waitress approached asking if they would like something from the bar. She left with an order for two glasses of wine.

"I've never been to this restaurant. The decor is well done," Kyria said as she laid her small purse on the table.

"I don't come often since it's pretty expensive. I wanted to make our first date special though."

The waitress came with their wine and they toasted to their evening and the future. A few minutes later Mark's cell phone rang. He nearly groaned when he saw it was the hospital. "I've got to take this. There's a resident on tonight and I told him to call if he had any questions. I'll go out to the foyer where there's more privacy."

Kyria sat looking more closely at the style of the decorating. She hadn't done anything since the explosion in the way of work, not even looking at decorating magazines or websites. Use of color and line in the bar had caught her eye and Mark's phone call enabled her to turn her attention to it without being rude.

"Hey, gorgeous. Why haven't I seen you here before?" A man had walked over from the bar.

"Maybe I didn't want to be seen." Kyria kept her tone flat not wanting to encourage the man.

"Oh, I would definitely have seen you."

"That's gratifying to know."

Another man approached and said, "Have you been abandoned by your date? It's hard to believe he'd do that to such a lovely lady."

Kyria mentally rolled her eyes. Did these guys really think those were good pickup lines? "No, he'll be back as soon as his call is finished."

The second man picked up her hand and kissed the back. Kyria pulled her hand back and laid it in her lap. "I'd never leave a beauty like you alone for a phone call."

"You probably don't have lives hanging in the balance, either." Just then she felt lips on her shoulder by her neck.

"The lovely lady is mine, boys, so I'd appreciate you stepping back to the bar," Mark said as he leaned down and kissed on her on the shoulder. Kyria's face flamed and she looked down as the men left.

"Why did you do that, Mark?" Kyria said through clenched teeth.

"What?"

"Kiss my shoulder."

"Just letting them know you weren't available."

"You couldn't simply return and sit down?"

"You don't understand guys. If I'd done that they wouldn't have known we were serious. I was making sure they understood you're mine."

"I am?"

"Yeah." Mark grinned at her.

"Oh." His comments made her feel superb, as if she belonged.

The hostess came then saying their table was ready. They ate dinner then Mark convinced Kyria to share a dessert with him. While waiting for the French silk pie she excused herself going to the ladies room.

As she walked back to the table she saw a woman seated in her chair. Deciding to be bold, Kyria slipped behind Mark, slid her arms over his shoulders and across his chest. Kissing his ear she said, "Someone you know, honey? Will you introduce me?" Kyria watched as his ears grew red.

"Um, this is Rita. She was keeping me company while you were gone. Thanks, Rita. Bye." Mark squirmed a little as Kyria kept hold of him and Rita got up and left.

Kyria let her hands glide across his chest and shoulders as she moved to sit down. Smiling, she took a sip of water looking at Mark's red face.

"I didn't invite her to the table. She just sort of sat down and started talking. I didn't want her to stay, but couldn't figure out how to get rid of her. I was just about to come find you when you came back." Mark's words spilled from his mouth like a speeding car. He had that deer in the headlights panicked look on his face.

Kyria reached across the table and patted his hand. "I think she got the message that you aren't quite available." At Mark's visible relaxation at her words she lifted her glass again to hide the smile tugging at her lips.

CHAPTER THIRTEEN

All he wanted was a cup of coffee. The surgery had been long and the case very touch and go. He'd assisted Keith Austin again. Mark had finally gotten through to him that the insinuations about Kyria had better stop or he'd need to find a different surgeon to assist on a regular basis. Keith and he made a good team and Keith knew it. He didn't want to lose Mark.

It had come to a head a couple of weeks prior. They had been in the locker room changing from their scrubs when Keith had asked Mark if he was still doing that little bomb victim. Unable to contain his rage Mark had pushed the man against the lockers.

"You insinuate one more time about Kyria and I'll not only refuse to do any more cases with you, but I just might make it so you need plastic surgery on that pretty face of yours. I won't tell you again. Nothing happened. I wouldn't disrespect any woman in that way. You have no clue about the circumstances and have believed gossip that's untrue.

"At one time I counted you as a friend. You've pushed me too far in this and I won't stand for another word. Kyria is a fine, respectable woman. She's done nothing to earn the slander that was spread about her.

"She's also my girlfriend and you will speak to me with respect about her. Have I made myself clear?"

"Hey, Mark. I didn't know you were serious about her. Sorry, man. Thought she was just another piece of…" Mark's growl cut Keith's comment off. "Okay, I get it. She's a great girl. Hope things go great with her. Good luck."

Mark let Keith go. He gritted his teeth and finished changing. It had taken several surgeries for the tension between them to lessen. Now they could work together comfortably, but outside of the operating room they seldom chatted or bantered as they had before.

He entered the employee lounge to get the desired coffee and was pouring the cup when arms went around his waist and a body, a female body, was pressed up against his back. Lips pressed against his neck and nibbled over to his ear.

"Hey, I know where we could go and have a sweet little interlude." Julie was obviously trying to sound sexy but to Mark it just sounded crass.

He set his cup and the coffee pot down and turned. She wrapped her arms more tightly around him and pressed her mouth to his. Mark wanted to spit. Instead he took hold of her arms and pushed her away.

"I'm only going to say this one time. You try this again and I'm going to Human Resources and report you for sexual harassment. I've got every time you've come on to me documented and I will let them know." After her fourth attempt at seduction he'd begun the list. "You and your actions disgust me. I don't and wouldn't ever want a women who acts like you. Now, leave me alone or I will go to HR."

"And I'd be a witness for him." Nurse Gadsden's voice made both Mark and Julie start and turn towards her. "If you want to lose your job, Julie, just keep doing what you're doing. I've seen and heard you come on to him several times and him rebuff you each time. Take your slutty ways and find someone who wants to roll in the gutter with you and leave Dr. Jenner alone."

Julie huffed and stalked from the lounge, her crocs squeaking as she went.

Mark looked at Nurse Gadsden. "Thank you. I appreciate you saying what you did."

"No problem, Doc. I have seen you push away her advances and heard her complain about your rejection. This time I was just in the right place at the right time to give you a helping hand. Maybe she'll leave you alone now."

Mark gave a wry grin. "I hope you're right. Threatening her

job just might do that. Wish I'd thought of it sooner. Thanks for the back up."

He handed her the cup of coffee he'd been pouring and poured another for himself. "Ms. Gadsden, I know you thought a lot of Kyria. I want you to know that nothing happened between her and me. Not that night I ended up staying there. She was ill and I didn't feel comfortable leaving her alone. You know how she never had any visitors."

"Yeah, poor thing. Never have seen a patient so alone."

Mark blew on the hot liquid and took a sip. "Yeah, well, Kyria and I, well, we're dating. I'm really interested in a relationship with her. I hate the gossip and rumors that have been spread about us. None of it was true. Well, I did stay over that one night but I slept on the couch, alone." He grinned a bit. "Well, her cats spent part of the night with me, or rather on me."

That elicited a chuckle from the nurse.

"After I confronted you about it, right after it happened, I got to thinking. I compared the person who was telling everyone and you. She's been known to gossip and isn't the most trustworthy in what she says and does. You, on the other hand, have always been honest and respectful. You don't tear other people down either to their face or behind their backs.

"As I thought about it I realized something just didn't jibe. Didn't measure up. Just didn't fit. I've never known you to take advantage of someone. And—" She winked at him. "I knew you were attracted to her even while she was in the hospital.

"I decided that there must be a different reality than what was being spread. So, I decided to give you the benefit of the doubt. Grace, you might say."

At the use of the word 'grace' Mark eyed her sharply. Most people who weren't believers would never use that term. They wouldn't understand what it meant.

"Yeah," Nurse Gadsden said. "I'm a believer. I don't wear it on my sleeve but try to live it." She glanced at the door Julie had exited through. "Tough enough around here to live it without having people throw it in your face when they sin and think you're judging them."

Mark nodded.

"Anyway, I just wanted to let you know I don't think you did anything to be ashamed of in helping Kyria. Heard you say you were dating her." Her brow furrowed and she shot him her typical disapproving look. "I'm warning you right now. If you hurt her I'll come up really ugly on you. She may not have any family and such but she's got me in her corner."

"Yes, ma'am. Duly warned."

Nurse Gadsden turned and carried her cup of coffee with her as she left the lounge.

CHAPTER FOURTEEN

They saw each other every day for the next few weeks. She was gaining strength but still required more rest than normal. Each time Kyria was more and more drawn to Mark and hoped and prayed he felt the same. Today he was going to take her to see his condo. He'd asked her to redecorate it for him. He warned her it was awful in its present state.

Kyria was waiting by the doorman's desk when Mark pulled up in his car. She hurried out and got in. Mark leaned over giving her a quick kiss before pulling away from the building.

"So, I'm finally going to see this monstrosity you bought."

"That's the perfect word for it. I love the layout and the view is great but, well you'll see. I wouldn't want to prejudice you before you see it."

Kyria laughed. "All you've done is complain about how awful it is since you mentioned it."

"Well, yeah. But it is."

Mark made her close her eyes before he opened the door. He pulled her into the condo with a warning not to peek as he closed it. "Okay, open."

Kyria opened her eyes and looked around the living area. She walked into the kitchen going through to the doorway at the other end. Then she went into each room before standing to look out the picture windows at the view.

"Well, you were absolutely correct in your assessment. This is truly awful. How could you buy such a place?"

"The view is wonderful and the price was loooow."

"That's good. Who lived here before? Some goth?"

"It is pretty dark and dreary. The price was low enough I figured I could have it totally redecorated and still have made a good bargain. So will you do it?"

"Where will you live while it's going on?" Kyria asked.

"What do you mean?"

"There's more than decorating you need done. I'm surprised they allowed the sale to go through. You shouldn't use the full bathroom. It's full of mold. You really shouldn't live here until it's remediated."

Mark stood stunned. He had mold? How could she tell? She'd just walked through each of the rooms in a few minutes. "I have mold? Show me."

Kyria led him to the bathroom and pointed to the area behind the toilet, along the wall by the shower and by the mirror. "The splatter paint hid it so it's hard for someone not used to seeing it to notice. I'm not sure how it passed inspection when you bought it. This entire room needs to be taken down to the studs and redone. The rest of the condo should be checked, too."

She went on to explain massive remodeling of the bathroom and kitchen evident to her trained eye in the cursory look she'd taken in her walk through. The bathroom had leaks and mold. The kitchen was in bad need of a total makeover. Kyria had some ideas to bring the condo into what she called 'the modern age' that she wanted to try.

"So I have to move out until it's done?"

"It would be best. You don't want to live in the mold."

"How long will it take?"

"Depends. Weeks, a couple of months. If you can't get a good contractor maybe longer."

Mark brightened. "I know a really good contractor who can do it all, and he won't take a long time." But where would he stay in the meantime. He looked at Kyria. Okay, Lord. I get it. Move me out of my place so now's the time. But he wouldn't propose in his moldy condo. He'd do it right. He also needed to talk with Hutch. He'd made Mark promise to let him know if he was going to.

There was a peace and rightness settling on him. Besides that,

Mark had the feeling he was already in love with her.

~~~~~

"Hi Hutch. I'm fulfilling my promise to contact you." Mark said after he'd dropped Kyria at her place. They'd had dinner where she began throwing out ideas for his condo. The whole thing overwhelmed him. It looked like he would have to make a million decisions. He'd gotten a hotel room for the night. He'd find something less expensive tomorrow.

"Oh?"

"Everything is going great with Kyria and God seems to be putting giant road signs pointing me to propose. I'm going to within the next week."

"What kind of road signs?" Hutch's voice was filled with caution. "Wait, let me go into my office. Chloe's looking at me like I'm nuts." Mark had called Hutch at home. He waited for his brother-in-law to pick up the extension. "Okay, shoot."

"Well, after I talked with you I went to Kyria's and we talked about doing some dating. We've been doing so ever since. Believe me, I've been praying about this whole thing. Kyria and I both have, together and separately." Mark picked the tennis ball off the bedside table and started tossing it in the air.

"I'm glad to hear that."

"We have so many things in common. Our faith, our sense of humor."

"Oh no," laughed Hutch.

"Yeah, do you believe it? We've gotten real close. And I'll tell only you, and don't you tell Chloe, but I've gotten really attracted to her, if you know what I mean."

"I know what you mean. Just be careful."

"Yeah, I know. Believe me, I know. Anyway, I took her to see my condo today. It was sort of God's way of saying it's time to make this official."

"How'd he do that?"

"Mold."

"Huh?"

"Kyria found mold in my condo. I'm sitting in a hotel, alone by the way, because she found mold in the bathroom. I'm stuck out of it until it can be taken care of. I'm not sure how long I'll be out. I'm going to get Dad and Luke to take a look at it and do the work, but I'll still be out until it's done."

"So?"

"If Kyria and I get married we can stay in her apartment together until it's finished."

"That is a stupid reason to propose."

"On the face of it yeah, but for the past couple of weeks I've been sure this is what God is wanting. My feelings for her have grown stronger. I've just been looking for that last little bit. That last nudge. I think mold in my condo is it. I've really come to admire Kyria for who she is. I'm pretty sure I'm in love with her. She's sweet, funny, smart, pretty, gaining weight."

"What?"

Mark laughed. "She lost so much when she was in the hospital she has to. None of her clothes fit and she had to buy a bunch so she had something besides sweats and boxers to wear."

"Oh," Hutch laughed. "Most men want skinny wives and you want yours to fatten up."

"She's not my wife yet. If she says yes, and doesn't want a huge hoopla of a wedding, we could tie the knot and live at her place while we redo mine."

"Well, you sound like a guy wanting to propose."

"If she says yes will you do the honors?"

"On one, no two conditions. One, you two come for pre-marital counseling and two, you talk with a lawyer about a prenup. Chloe and I signed one and with the company, you should, too."

"Sounds reasonable. I hope she doesn't get upset about it."

"If she does, you need to head the other way. Prenups are pretty common these days," Hutch said.

"I don't plan to get a divorce no matter what. Marriage isn't just between the couple, it's a covenant with God."

"Right, most people don't think of it that way. They just hit a rocky patch and give up. It takes hard work to be married and harder to be married happily."

After finishing the call, Mark thought about Hutch's comments about the work of marriage and figured the preacher probably knew what he was talking about. He was busy counseling married couples all the time.

He shifted his thought to how to ask and about rings. Should he get the rings or have her go with him? When and how should he ask? How could he get her to skip the big honking wedding and just have a small quick one?

~~~~~

Saturday was a bright sunny May day. Kyria was finishing getting ready for her day with Mark. They were going to the botanical gardens, then for lunch. As usual, before she was done with her make-up the doorbell rang. Now she just opened the door and headed back to the bathroom to finish.

"So I'm early again, huh?" Mark said leaning against the bathroom doorframe.

"You always are. I should probably start at least fifteen minutes early getting ready before you come."

"Why don't you, if you know I'm going to come early?"

"Cause I like to sleep. I'd have to get up earlier if I did."

"That doesn't work for afternoon or evening dates."

Kyria dropped the mascara back into the draw, shut it, turned to him and playfully pushed his shoulder. "How do you know? Maybe I sleep all day before I see you."

"A little sleep, a little slumber…"

"I know but I am still recovering you know."

"Yeah, yeah, yeah. How long are you going to play that one out?"

"Until my doctor releases me."

"Well…"

"Not you. My real doctor."

"I'm a real doctor."

Kyria didn't say anything. Grabbing her sweater and purse, she led the way from the apartment.

~~~~~

"Aren't these colors lovely?" Kyria asked as they strolled through the beds of annuals.

"Too much pink for my taste."

"These are what I'm thinking for your living room." Kyria teased.

"Yeah, uh huh. Come, let's sit on the bench by that fountain."

Mark placed his hand on the small of her back guiding her to the bench. She loved how the small gesture made her feel. Cared for, protected, almost loved. They sat watching the glistening water shoot high, sprinkling into the pool. Kyria loved fountains. Someday, she wanted a house with a fountain inside.

"Kyria." Mark pulled her attention to him. "I've come to care for you so very much. I hope you feel the same." She nodded, her heart thumping when he paused. "It's been on my thoughts for a while that I want you in my life always."

Now Kyria's hands began to shake. Mark pulled a small velvet box from his pocket and held it out to her. "I love you. Will you marry me?"

He opened the box. Kyria stared, her eyes going wide, tears filled them. It must be some sort of cruel joke. She brought a hand up and bit the knuckle of her index finger. Wasn't she even worth the traditional engagement ring?

"What's wrong? Have I misread your feelings?" Mark wrapped her in his arms.

"If you want to marry me, why is the box empty?" Kyria's voice cracked with a sob.

Mark realized his plan had backfired. He'd thought they'd laugh over the empty ring box, go to the jewelers and pick out a set they both liked. He reached out and pulled her to him, holding her tightly.

"Oh honey, I'm sorry. I love you. I do want to marry you. I just want us to pick out the rings together. Please say yes."

"Yes," Kyria said against his shoulder. Then she pulled back and slugged that same shoulder. "You meanie. I'd love to pick out rings with you."

Mark grabbed her face and kissed her throughly. "You had me scared for a minute. I thought you were going to say no. Let's skip the rest of the gardens and head to the jeweler's and pick them out."

This time Kyria grabbed his face and kissed him.

~~~~~

Later, they lay together on her sofa, Mark behind her, Kyria's back against his chest. She was holding her left hand up looking at the empty place on her ring finger.

"Isn't it just lovely? Thank you so much." The rings they'd picked out had to be sized and it would take several days.

Mark laughed. "Playing the invisible ring thing just a bit much, aren't you?"

"Hey, you started it. That box was either empty or had an invisible ring in it."

He laughed again and pressed her down so he could reach her lips. Desire flooded through him. He really needed to get out of there. Temptation was clawing at his insides.

"Babe, I hate to break this up but I really need to get out of here." He gave her a quick kiss. "You're heating me up and—"

Kyria pressed her figures to his lips. "I get it. Just so you know I feel the same way." She rolled off the sofa and onto her feet.

Mark noted that she was moving more easily now. Her recovery was still slow but progressing.

CHAPTER FIFTEEN

That evening after Mark left, heading back to the cheap motel with the monthly, weekly, nightly and hourly rates, Kyria called Russ Naylor, her lawyer. She was very excited about her news, but maintained the calm demeanor she'd been trained to have.

"Uncle Russ, I've some news for you. I've been dating Dr. Mark Jenner and today he asked me to marry him."

"Well, well, well. If you are calling me, I guess that means you said yes."

Losing some of her composure as the excitement bubbled she said, "Yes, and I'm so happy. We've decided to have a small wedding in as short a time as possible since his condo has mold and he can't live in it until it's fixed."

"Not the most romantic reason to get married, but if it works for you," Russ teased.

Kyria laughed. "You know what I mean. Not a reason to get married, but logical for getting married soon."

"We'll have to get together and develop a prenuptial agreement. It's a wise thing to do and a stipulation of the trust. Do you think he'll have any problem with that?"

"I don't think so, but we didn't discuss it today. When we're together tomorrow, I'll bring it up."

"Good. I'll start on the preliminaries and meet with you both and his lawyer whenever you want. I'm going to be in the country for about six weeks, then gone for at least three. Have you made any plans for this quickie wedding?"

"Not yet. I'll let you know as soon as we make any decisions."

"One more thing." She could hear the love he had for her in his voice.

"What?"

"May I give you away?"

"Oh, Uncle Russ," Kyria lost all composure now and with tears streaming down her face said, "I'd love you to."

~~~~~

Mark was surprised the next day after worship service, as they ate lunch, when Kyria brought up the topic of a prenup. He'd been worried she would object and here she was wanting one of her own.

"I was going to ask if you would sign one," Mark said biting into his big burger. "My family has a construction business which we all have part ownership in. It's standard for each of us kids to get one to protect the business. Dad and Luke own the most since they work it, but the rest of us kids have parts, too. They are who I'm going to talk to about remodeling the condo."

"I don't have any problem with signing one for you if you don't have one for signing a prenup for me. I have a trust set up by my folks. One of the stipulations is a prenup."

"Well, that was easy. I'll talk to my lawyer. Since I presume your Uncle Russ will handle yours, we can have them get together about it." Mark was relieved at how smoothly the issue was handled. "So, when do you want to have the wedding and where and all that stuff?"

"Uncle Russ wants to give me away. I was so moved when he asked me if he could." Mark saw a hint of moisture in her eyes. "He has to leave the country in six weeks. Do you think it's possible to have the wedding by then?"

"So you can't wait to have your wicked way with me?" Mark closed one eye nearly all the way giving her an evil grin.

"It's not wicked if we're married." Kyria popped a catsup laden french fry into her mouth.

"Do you want the wedding at the church? Oh, my brother-in-law Hutch, who's a pastor, wants to officiate. Is that okay with you?" Kyria gave him an odd look. "I hope you don't mind. Our relationship happened so fast I've talked to him a couple of times wanting some spiritual counsel."

Kyria was silent for a few moments causing Mark to worry that it bothered her.

"I think it was wise of you. It must be comforting knowing you can talk to someone about things."

The comment struck Mark as odd, then he remembered how alone she had been while in the hospital. He reached over and stroked her face gently. "You have me to talk with about anything." He was touched when she turned her face into his palm and kissed it.

"Thank you."

"On that note. You seemed nervous or agitated in service today. Any reason? Remember you can talk to me about anything." He watched as Kyria seemed to struggle with an answer.

"Um, yeah. I, uh, felt awkward today. I called the woman in charge of the Children's Ministry to let her know why I hadn't been there to help and to tell her I still wasn't able. She, um, told me, um, that she couldn't have me work with the kids anymore since I was of questionable moral character. My OD'ing on the pain meds must have gotten back to her."

Mark regretted bringing it up. They'd been planning the wedding and having fun doing so, and now he'd brought sadness to her face. Pastor McCachron had called and warned him if any other incidents concerning Mark were brought to his attention he'd be asked to step down from his position on the addiction support team. He didn't know if their engagement would change anything but figured that with the quick wedding the worst would still be thought.

"Kyria, I don't think your OD'ing was what caused you to be kicked off the Children's ministry team. I think that was my fault."

"What? Why?" Her confusion made him feel awful.

"You know I spent the night taking care of you. I slept on the couch. In the morning I took a shower and hadn't buttoned my shirt yet when the doorbell rang. I thought it was your building super. Instead it was several ladies from church bringing food for you. Seems after I contacted them about why you hadn't been there they asked for people to do that." He swallowed not wanting to continue but she needed to know. He hated that. All he wanted to do was protect her from hurt. Now he was going to cause her hurt and, unfortunately, they were in a public place.

"Babe, the ladies thought I had spent the night with you, in the Biblical sense. I didn't even think about explaining that you were ill. I was being a stupid male and just oblivious to the whole thing."

Kyria's gaze dropped from his face to the table. Her hands disappeared beneath it onto her lap. "Why didn't you tell me?"

"At first, I didn't think about it. I knew nothing happened. It never occurred to me that others might see things in a different light. Then when it started spreading through the hospital—"
Her gasp made him stop. Oh man, he'd been oblivious again.

"What has been spread through the hospital?" The tremor in her voice gripped his heart with tight fist.

"Um, at least one of the ladies who brought food told about finding me at your apartment. They put the worst possible spin on it."

"So they're talking about me, right?" Her voice had gotten weaker.

"Um." He hesitated. Each word seemed to stab her and he didn't know if he could wound her more. "There has been some. About me, too."

"But with men it's different. They look at you as the conquering stud. Me, they look at as a slut."

He saw a tear fall from her face to the table. She looked so defeated. He reached across the table and tapped her arm. She lifted her hand and he took it in his. "We can't control what other people do or say. We can only control our own tongues and actions. We know the truth. We live knowing that truth and let the shield of our faith extinguish the arrows shot at us."

"I think you've messed that verse up a little. It's arrows of the evil one that get extinguished." The corner of her mouth turned up just a bit. It gave him heart to continue.

"Who's to say that isn't what this is? Something the evil one devised to break us apart. He's not above doing that."

"No, he's not." She paused, then looked up at him. "Mark, don't keep things like this from me again. You told me before that

I have you to talk to now about anything. How can I trust enough to do that if you don't tell me things that affect my life? I know you were trying to protect me, but that's not what it feels like."

He drew his brows together trying to figure out what she meant.

"I was raised wrapped in bubble wrap. They were trying to protect me from any possible hurt. In reality they were smothering me. I struggle at times to deal with the most mundane things. Rather than helping me learn to manage and overcome the hurts and challenges of life they tried to shield me from all of it. In doing so I became an adult not even being able to cross the street alone and buy a sandwich."

It hit him then. She wasn't crying because of the gossip. Well, that was part of it, he was positive. She was more upset because he didn't trust her to be able to handle it. He'd tried to wrap her in bubble wrap, as she put it, and protect her from hurt.

"I'm sorry. You're right. My motive might have been right but I handled it wrong. You're a grown woman who can deal with the talk. You know you, we, didn't do anything wrong. I should have come and told you as soon as I heard about the gossip."

She used her free hand to pick a napkin out of the container and blow her nose. Then she gave a watery smile. "You're forgiven." She shot him a firm look, one that reminded him of his mother's most serious expression. "Don't let it happen again."

"Yes ma'am."

They ate silently for a while then Mark said, "How about we start looking for a different church? Pastor McCachron's messages aren't changing many lives. It's too bad. I like him."

"Let's think about it. We can see how things go after a while. I'd hate to leave just because someone hurt my feelings. Look how much the Jews hurt Jesus but he didn't leave them."

"No, they left him."

CHAPTER SIXTEEN

"How about having the wedding at my folks house? It's large and the yard is big enough. You've said you only have a few people you'd like to invite and it would make it easy for my family not to have to travel here." After leaving the restaurant they'd gone to the park where Mark had proposed. They were sitting on the same bench near the fountain.

"To say nothing about trying to find a venue in this short of time. I like that idea, if you don't think they'd mind."

"You've got to be joking. My mother loves to have parties. Her last child getting married will give her the opportunity to throw a big one." When Kyria's eyes opened wide Mark said, "Not big in numbers but big."

They spent the rest of the afternoon choosing colors; yellow and red, cake flavors; red velvet and white since Mark said his mother would demand two, and the guest list; just immediate family on Mark's side; Uncle Russ, Amisa and her family, Steve, her building super, along with his family and Mamie, Kyria's nanny, if she could make it. Kyria would send her the plane tickets.

They picked up a pizza and went back to her apartment. After they'd eaten Mark said they needed to call his folks. All his siblings and their families would be there. Kyria was nervous. What would they say? She and Mark hadn't been dating long.

"Hi Dad, will you put this on speaker phone. I only want to say this one time." Kyria smacked Mark on the knee. He kissed her cheek. A bunch of 'Hi's' and 'Hey Mark's' could be heard.

"Must be most of you there," Mark said.

"All but you, little bro." The voice was male.

"That's my older brother, Luke," Mark whispered.

"Well, how about if I come up next weekend?"

"Sounds good to us," Mark's Dad said. "We always love to see you."

"Do you mind if I bring someone along?"

"No, bring anyone you want." A female voice.

"That's my mom," Mark whispered again. "Listen to this reaction." He paused then said, "It's my fiancé." Screams and screeches could be heard through the speaker. "Something wrong there?" Mark grinned at Kyria, squeezing her hand.

"No, Mark, no. My final child finds a bride and doesn't even tell us he's been dating. I love it," his mother said.

"Hutch knew."

"You told him and you didn't tell me?" Luke broke in.

"He's my best friend."

"I'm your brother."

"Yeah, so."

"Mark, is she with you? What's her name?"

"Yes, and Kyria. You want to talk to her?" Mark held the phone closer to her. Kyria's eyes went wide.

"Hello, Kyria, I can't wait to meet you. I love you already if you love my son. Make him bring you up here early next weekend. Plan to spend it here. We have plenty of space."

"Hello, Mrs. Jenner. I look forward to meeting you also. You've raised a wonderful son."

"Don't Mrs. Jenner me. It's Heather or Mom, whichever you prefer."

"Mom," Mark said. "May we have the wedding at the house?" More screams came from the speaker. "In maybe three or four weeks?"

"Three weeks? Mark?" The disapproval came through loud and clear. It was obvious what his mother thought.

"No! It's not that, Mrs. Jenner. I'm not pregnant." Kyria grabbed the phone as she spoke. "It's the mold."

"What?"

"Mom," Mark took the phone back. "I'll send an email explaining the whole thing to all of you. But we still would like the wedding in three weeks. Hutch," Mark called the name louder.

"Yeah, buddy. Congratulations by the way."

"Can we get all the prenup classes done in three weeks?"

"It'll take some doing, as well as Skyping, but we should be able to. Call me tomorrow and we can set up a schedule. Hi Kyria, I've heard a lot about you. I look forward to meeting you."

"As do I."

"Well guys, I'm going to hang up now. We can talk next weekend when we get there," Mark said. A chorus of well wishes and byes were heard then he cut the connection. "That wasn't so bad now, was it." They were on the sofa in her apartment in their usual casual position; Kyria leaning back against Mark's chest.

"How many people were there? It sounded like a hundred."

"Do you want it counting kids or just adults?"

"Adults."

"Eight unless my grandparents are there, then there'd be ten. My mom's folks. But a lot of the noise was probably the kids. Six kids between two and six years old."

"Oh my, that's a big family. There are only my brother and me, and I haven't a clue where he is."

"It's so hard for me to think that you don't know where he is. I know where everyone is, at least in general."

"We aren't very close. Turner is six years older." Kyria didn't say anything else.

~~~~~

By Wednesday the lawyers had gotten together and drawn up the pre-nuptial documents. Mark picked Kyria up after he got off his shift at two o'clock. Traffic was heavy so Mark decided to bring up something that had concerned him.

"Kyria, I don't want you to be uncomfortable, especially in my folks house. They've done real well and the house is very nice and quite large. They do own a construction company after all. I figure they'll put you in the bedroom next to theirs and me upstairs in my old room. It's multilayered down a slope."

"You don't need to be concerned that I'll be intimidated by a large house. I've decorated a number of them. My parent's home was relatively large, too. We sold it after they died."

"Did it hurt to have to sell it?" Mark figured it must have hurt to have to sell a family home.

"No, not really. I wasn't in it much."

Mark wanted to quiz her, but had to turn into the parking garage just then. He knew they wouldn't get another chance to talk about it until after the meeting and hoped it wouldn't be hard for her to see his net worth.

They went over the documents she would sign first. There were provisions for her if he passed away, for children from the marriage, what she would receive if they divorced. Mark watched Kyria as she read them. She asked a few questions, then asked her Uncle Russ if he approved. When he said it was all in order she picked up a pen and signed. Kyria then turned the papers for his signature.

When both lawyers were satisfied, Russell Naylor handed him Kyria's prenup for him to read. When Mark saw the value of her trust he swallowed. Boy, had his impression of her been way off. The net worth of her trust, without mention of her brother's, was more than three times the value of the entire Jenner Construction Company.

Kyria was wealthy beyond what most people ever dreamed of. Why hadn't she said anything? More than that, why was she living in such a small apartment in not so good of a neighborhood? She shopped sales, had a small not so new car and had urged him not to get as large a diamond for her ring as he wanted. He'd won that battle.

Now he finds out she could buy and sell his entire family several times over. They hadn't really talked about money. Kyria had a job as a decorator waiting for her. He knew he had to make more money than she did, but why did she even work. Kyria didn't have to work to support herself. Even though she wouldn't have had to work after they were married since he could support her, she'd told him she wanted to continue with the decorating.

Mark pushed all that aside and read the documents. The same sort of issues had been covered by Russ in these papers as by his lawyer. An amount had even been included to be paid to him if he became disabled and unable to work. Much of the trust would go to the 'issue of her body,' namely any children they had, but the amount left to him was still staggering.

When Mark finished he looked at his lawyer who nodded his approval. Mark signed. He stood silently as Kyria spoke to Russ about the wedding details. Russ kissed her on the cheek promising to be there ready, willing and able, in time for the rehearsal. Shaking hands with both lawyers and placing his hand on Kyria's back he guided her to the elevator and down to the parking garage.

"You're very quiet," Kyria said once they were buckled in their seat. Mark took his hand off the key before he started the car.

"I'm just stunned. Why didn't you tell me?"

"Tell you what?"

"Well, that you're filthy rich I suppose. That you can buy and sell my family several times and still have plenty left over."

"Oh, I didn't think it mattered. It's just money. I give a lot of it away."

"Okay, I know I come from a fairly well off family. I've not known want in my life. My family has a very nice house, or houses since we're all supporting ourselves now."

"With the exception of you," Kyria interjected.

"I support myself." Mark turned on the car and headed out to the street

"But your home is awful... moldy, too."

Mark chuckled at her teasing. "You're right, but I'm working on it."

"No, your dad and brother are or will be soon anyway." Her deadpan comment made him laugh.

"I'm busy at the hospital. I'm a doctor not a builder. But still, why do you live so modestly if you have so much money?"

"If people know you have money they treat you differently. I don't want to be known for having a bunch of money. I don't like the rich people scene. It's very fake. Fake people, fake smiles, fake bodies, fake friends. I have to do it sometimes, charity galas and stuff like that. I do as little as I can get away with."

"You think if people here knew how much you were worth

they would treat you differently?"

Kyria turned in her seat to look at him. "Do you think if the pastor or the ladies at church knew I had money they would have kicked me off the children's ministry team?"

Mark thought about it. He'd simply been warned not to let anything happen again to jeopardize his work with the addicted. They knew that not only he was a respected physician, but also the son of the Jenner Construction Company owner. Kyria seemed to have little money and no connections. The difference struck him.

"I see what you mean. They wouldn't want to risk the donations you might make to the church." Mark frowned as he turned a corner.

"Bingo. People get weird if they know you have money. I wouldn't want to have to figure out if someone wanted to be with me because of who I am or because of the money."

"Did I make a fool of myself telling you about my folks' big nice house?" He asked.

"Do you think you did?"

"I'm not sure."

"Remember one thing."

"What?"

"I've seen your condo."

CHAPTER SEVENTEEN

Chapter

Mark turned the car into the lane leading to his parent's house. He glanced at Kyria seated next to him. "Don't worry, they'll love you. We're a pretty easy family to get along with."

"I'm not nervous."

"Liar," Mark chuckled.

"Okay. I am nervous. You have such a large family. I'm not used to being around families. I'm not sure I know how to make conversation. I don't know anyone but you."

"Oh, don't worry." Now he was laughing. "They'll just keep asking you questions so the conversation will be easy."

"What?" The shriek nearly pierced his eardrum.

That sobered him. She really was nervous. Stopping the car in front of the house, Mark put it in park and then took her hand. "You'll be fine. I'm going to stay right next to you the whole day and fend my family off with a scalpel if need be. All right?"

Kyria let out a huge sigh. "All right. I'm going to hold you to it."

Mark squeezed her hand before they opened their doors and got out. He looked at the house when he heard the front door open and saw his family pouring out. Hurrying around the car he slipped his arm around Kyria who was standing stock still watching everyone flood toward them.

"Okay, group," he called. "We need air, so keep back a little. I don't want my fiancé running away or passing out from fear of the mob. She's from a small family so doesn't understand your enthusiasm."

The adults slowed their approach but the children continued running, hollering, "Uncle Mark, Uncle Mark." Soon he was surrounded by boys and girls ranging in age from six to two. He knelt down giving each a hug, picking up the youngest boy.

"Hey guys," Mark said. "I want you to meet my girlfriend. Her name's Kyria Metcalf. I'm going to marry her and then she'll be your Aunt Kyria. Isn't she pretty?" He looked at her, pleased when she blushed and swatted his arm lightly. "This young man is Grayson. He's two and belongs to Gavin and Trina." He set the boy down and proceeded to introduce the rest of his nieces and nephews.

~~~~~

Kyria watched as the children ran off after they'd been introduced. How was she ever going to put the names to the correct face? And those twins. They were identical. She'd always call them by the wrong one, she was sure. Feeling Mark pull on her hand she followed as he led her to the group of adults standing on the lawn.

"Mom, Dad, all the rest of you, I present Kyria Metcalf, my fiancé. Now, there are some ground rules before you swamp her with love and affection.

"Be careful, she's still recovering from an awful injury so don't hug her too hard. Don't be the Spanish Inquisition bombarding her with questions. I plan to have her around a long lifetime so there's time to learn all about her. Don't think you're going to get her alone to quiz her because," he held up their joined hands. "I superglued our hands together. You're just going to have to deal with me."

Kyria was surprised at his speech and more surprised when the family all laughed. She would never have said anything like that to her parents. Suddenly she was enveloped in a hug from the woman who must be Mark's mother.

"I'm Heather and I'm so glad to meet you. Mark sent us an email with a lot about you and I love you already."

Kyria could hear the sincerity in her voice and gave her a one handed hug. It was all she could do since Mark, good to his word, still held her hand.

"She loved you before she met you since you've succeeded in getting the final son to commit to someone." An older version of Mark replaced Heather wrapping his arms around her. "I'm Will, his dad, if you haven't guessed. Welcome to the family."

Each sibling and their spouses repeated the welcome as Mark introduced them. Luke, the oldest, and his wife Rachel. They had Brian, six and Grace, three. Gavin and Trina were parents of the six-year-old twins Kirk and Hart, towheaded Natalie, who was four, and the two-year-old, Grayson. Putting his arm around a very pregnant young woman, Mark introduced Chloe, the lone girl of the siblings, and her husband Hutch.

Kyria smiled at each, praying she'd be able to pair the correct wife and husband and their children. Remembering names had always been a problem for her, one she had worked to improve without much success. Her parents had not been pleased with her failure. She so wanted to be accepted by Mark's family. If she couldn't remember their names they would hate her for sure.

"We've got lunch all prepared. Let's go in, eat and talk about the wedding," Mark's mother said.

As they talked about the wedding it became apparent three weeks wouldn't be enough. With Russ Naylor leaving the country in six that set a definite deadline if he was going to give her away. Heather took charge and laid out a plan that, if all her daughters-in-law and daughter helped, they could get everything done for the wedding to be held in a month.

Kyria had brought samples of the colors they'd chosen which all the ladies loved. The men teased Mark that they should have chosen green to represent jealousy, instead of red, and the yellow was a stripe down his back.

Conversation then centered around the menu for the reception. Pulled pork sandwiches, potato and other salads as well as other suggestions were made, some good, others only intended to bring a laugh.

To Kyria, the patio where they ate seemed to be in constant motion. Between the children eating, shouting and running, and parents laughing, eating and chasing children, the noise and movement began to wear.

Mark noticed her sagging, and when it looked like she'd eaten all she wanted, he stood up and said, "As my fiancé's doctor in residence, I proclaim she is in need of a respite from this loud obnoxious family. We are going to the sunroom so she can rest, and since we are superglued together," Mark grabbed her hand in his and held them up, "I will have to stay with her while she naps. Please observe quiet time."

Mark started to lead Kyria away when he heard his four year old niece Grace say, "Aunt Kyria takes a nap, too? I thought she'd be too old for naps."

"We're never too old for naps," Gavin, Mark's next older brother said, scooping up his daughter. "How about you and me taking one together." Squeals of delight followed Mark and Kyria into the house.

~~~~~

Mark watched as Kyria looked around the sunroom. Large, with two walls of windows, the room lived up to its name. Wicker furniture and giant pillows gave it a relaxed tropical feel. A wide couch faced the windows looking out on a pond with a fountain in the middle shooting water at least twenty feet high. Mark opened windows on both walls so they could hear the fountain and birds.

"Come, lie down here with me." He indicated the couch as he picked up an afghan. "You look tired."

"I am, but should we?" She looked at the door he'd closed.

"It's not a problem, see." He pointed out the window. Several adults and the three six-year-old boys were just out of earshot starting a game of some sort of ball. "I picked this room because it gives us just enough privacy and just enough visibility. You can bet my mother sent them there specifically."

Kyria relaxed, kicked off her shoes and crawled onto the couch so she could see out the window. Mark settled behind her, covering them both with the blanket.

"So are you overwhelmed?" Mark asked smoothing her hair away from his face.

"A little. I've not been around families much. We were kept out of the way when my parents had friends over, my brother and I. When they went somewhere we were usually left at home until we were older."

"You must have been lonely."

"Maybe, I don't really know. It was just the way it was. I didn't know any other way."

Mark started to ask another question when Kyria jerked and pointed.

"Oh look."

Mark lifted his head and saw one of the twins standing, soaking wet, knee-deep in the pond. He chuckled as the others all laughed. Then Gavin threw the other twin, he couldn't tell which was which from this distance, into the water. "Watch." He kissed Kyria's ear.

Luke picked up his son and charged into the water, bumping into Gavin, managing to knock him down. The two women stood nearby shaking their heads and laughing. Soon they started running as the now soaked men came chasing after their wives.

"What are they chasing them for? Are they angry about their laughing?" Kyria was tense in his arms.

"No." Just then Luke caught Rachel lifting her high while all the boys cheered. Rachel's shrieks came in the open windows along with her laughter and screams of 'no'. Luke strode into the pond then tossed his wife in. Gavin had caught Trina and she landed next to Rachel who had come up sputtering.

Mark began to chuckle rubbing Kyria's arm. "It's all right. They're just playing around. Chloe is only exempt because she's so pregnant."

The wrestling in the water went on for a while with the three boys helping their mothers push their dads back into the pond. When the show ended with the soaking wet participants trooping toward the house Mark felt Kyria finally relax.

"I take it your parents didn't fool around much," Mark said.

"No, never."

He wondered what kind of childhood she'd had. Whenever Kyria spoke of her parents it was in a very neutral tone. The nanny, Mamie, she spoke of lovingly. Maybe Kyria was one of those rich kids he'd heard about whose parents simply left them for servants to raise.

Mark continued to stroke her arm even after he knew she'd

fallen asleep. In a month he'd be able to not only nap in a very visible room but be with her in a very private one.

~~~~~

Kyria woke up alone. She'd felt secure falling to sleep in Mark's arms. There was a ball game going on near the pond which included Mark. She watched for a while trying to figure out what they were playing. It seemed the purpose was for the children to attack whoever had the ball as it was tossed between the men. Mark's brother's wives were helping the children by tackling their husbands. Hutch and the brothers tackled Mark whenever he had the ball. The abandon with which they ran and laughed was intriguing to Kyria. She'd never seen her parents or their friends relax in such a way.

When she went outside Kyria found Mark's parents and Chloe sitting on the patio watching, chatting with smiles on their faces. "Hello," Kyria said.

Will, Mark's father, rose offering his chair to Kyria, pulling another over for himself. "Did you have a nice nap?"

"Yes, thank you. It's a most beautiful room and the view is wonderful. The couch is very comfortable." Kyria smiled at each person.

"I planned the view with the large grassy area for the children to play where I could watch them and let them have fun thinking I couldn't see them. Several times I was downstairs by the time one came running to say somebody'd gotten hurt." Heather's eyes shone with fond memories.

"As we got older we figured out what you were doing. Most of the time we didn't care, but when we did we'd move that way," Chloe pointed toward the other end of the pond. "Then we'd be out of her view."

Will and Heather laughed. "So you thought," Will said. "What looks over that area?"

"Oh," moaned Chloe. "Mom's sitting room off your bedroom."

"You all thought you were so smart." Heather laughed. "But enough of that, if you're refreshed enough, Kyria, let's talk about the wedding. We don't have much time. Mark emailed me your guest list. Are you sure you don't want to invite anyone else, even though it's short notice?"

"No."

"I thought Mark said you had a brother," Will said.

"I do, but I don't know where he is." Kyria felt the aloneness she'd lived with for so long. Maybe, maybe Mark's family would accept her. She'd do her best to fit in.

Heather cleared her throat, obviously nervous. "Would it be all right if I made a few suggestions?"

"Of course," Kyria said knowing she'd take every one. "You've been through weddings before. I've not been involved in any." She saw Chloe and Heather exchange glances. What were they thinking? Anxiety rose within her.

"Well, you let me know if there's anything you don't like or have another idea about. It is your wedding." Heather reached over and patted Kyria's knee.

"Yes, ma'am."

"What do you think about being married in front of the pond? The fountain would make a beautiful background."

"Yes, it would. What if it rains?" It was a wonderful idea, Kyria thought. She already loved the view.

"That's why we had so many boys, they can move furniture in the living room. It's large enough to fit everyone. We've had more in there for parties before," Will said.

"We'll rent chairs. The church has a portable sound system so everyone will be able to hear," Chloe said.

"You all go to Hutch's church?" Kyria asked.

"Yes, it's the one we've gone to forever it seems," Will said. "He's brought a new style and bluntness of preaching which is attracting many new people."

They spent some time discussing the church before Heather brought them back to the wedding. "Okay, do you have a dress?"

Kyria thought for a moment. "I have a dress which will work. It's not a traditional wedding dress but it's white and long. I'll try it on this Monday to see if it needs altering. I've gained some weight back but I'm still thinner than I was."

"What about attendants?" Chloe asked.

Kyria thought about her lack of friends, Amisa came to mind. "I haven't asked anyone yet. I have someone in mind. I'll speak to her Monday as well. We can find a dress in the city, I'm sure."

Chloe laughed. "I'm sure it will be better than a bridesmaid's dress since you don't have time to order one. Prom dresses will be on sale now." All four of them laughed. There'd been several TV news features on lately spotlighting the fashions for the spring dances.

Kyria thought all the ideas Heather and Chloe came up with were wonderful, very much in tune with her taste. Simple spring flowers for the bouquets and reception centerpieces. The menu for the reception had been settled on at lunch. Soon Heather had divided all the tasks which needed doing, making lists for each person to complete.

The ball players came straggling in panting from their exertions, the men and children collapsing in the grass. Rachel and Trina accepting the chairs Will pulled into the conversation area.

"You looked like you were all having fun," Chloe said. "Soon I'll be able to join you."

The discussion shifted to Chloe's due date and what the baby's sex might be. Kyria listened to the teasing affection the siblings and their spouses had for each other. She hoped one day she'd feel comfortable enough to join in. Funny, she'd been able to tease Mark since she'd first met him.

Kyria watched him lying on his back trying to catch his breath. Then he turned over, lifted his head and smiled at her. He kissed the air as if sending her one. She smiled and wished she felt confident enough to reach out and catch it but didn't want to draw attention to herself by the motion. Her parents disapproved of such actions. Staying still when conversation was going on around her had been drilled in at a very young age.

Mark's nieces and nephews hadn't had that kind of teaching. Though they didn't interrupt, much, several climbed up in their parent's or grandparent's laps. Each was welcomed and wrapped in loving arms as the conversation continued around them.

Finally, one of the nieces, Kyria wasn't certain of her name, who was sitting on Heather's lap reached up putting both hands on her grandmother's cheeks and said, "I's hungry."

Heather gave the girl a hug. "I'll just bet you are. How about all you stinky ball players go get showered so you don't smell up the kitchen and by then I'll have the supper out and ready to eat?"

Gavin's twins and Luke's son, Brian, jumped and ran into the house yelling they got the mudroom shower. Their fathers followed to help. Mark whispered it would most likely be a communal one for the boys. He and the wives and girls went in to shower in other bathrooms.

"May I help get supper ready?" Kyria asked.

Heather gave her a quick hug. "Of course. Next time you'll probably be showering, too, since Mark will drag you into the game. Come on."

Kyria couldn't imagine playing such a rough and tumble game.

CHAPTER EIGHTEEN

"Your family is a little overwhelming," Kyria said the next afternoon as she and Mark drove back to the city. "I've never been around such an active group of people."

Mark smiled. "We are a big, loud, rambunctious group of people."

"You are definitely right, there," Kyria laughed. "It's so different from how my brother and I were raised. Of course, there were never any other children around. Only adults and they didn't really want to have us playing nearby."

Mark became serious. He'd wondered about her childhood and parents but Kyria never seemed to want to talk about them more than a word or two. "Where did you grow up?"

"Let's see, I was born in Connecticut. I've lived in Switzerland, France, England, Venezuela, Greece, Italy, the Philippines, California, Texas, Japan. I think that's all. Maybe some other places before I can remember."

"Wow, you moved a lot. My folks built the house when Chloe was born so we moved there, but nowhere else."

"We had houses or penthouses everywhere we went. Sometimes we'd travel some and be other places for short times. Those don't count, not really. We'd only stay there a month or two before going back to, well, whatever spot my parents either wanted or needed to go for business."

"What about when you went to school? Did you stay in one place then?"

"No. We had a tutor who traveled with us. We'd study the country or city we were in. Go to the museums, parks, cultural centers. Some would say it was an enviable education. I suppose it was. I think it has helped in my decorating, having seen so many styles and color schemes."

Mark thought for a moment. Kyria sat looking out the window next to him. "What about other kids, playmates?"

"It was only Turner and me. He left when I was ten. He graduated early and went on a world tour before starting college at seventeen."

How lonely Kyria must have been. It was so foreign to the way he had grown up. His folks loved to entertain and nearly always included the families of those they invited. There would be activities for the children and for the adults also, if they wanted to participate. Neighborhood kids had often been at the Jenner house. His mother always made sure there were plenty of fruit, crackers and other snacks available. Often one or more of their friends would stay for supper or overnight. Sometimes the Jenner children did the same at their friends' houses.

"When did your parents die?"

"Just after my twenty-fourth birthday, maybe two months. My father was flying them from England to New York in their jet. Something went wrong and they crashed on Greenland trying to do an emergency landing."

"That must have been hard for you." He reached over to hold her hand.

"I suppose. Mamie came and stayed with me, so that made it okay. Turner was back for about three weeks. It was good to see him."

"He's what, six years older than you?"

"Yes."

"And you don't have much contact?"

"No. Occasionally, he emails. Last I knew he was mountain climbing in Africa."

No family but an absent brother, an uncle who wasn't really one but the lawyer who dealt with her trust, and a nanny. They were the only people she'd mentioned whenever they talked about friends or family. No wonder no one had called while she was in the hospital.

"Is Mamie still alive?"

"Yes, she lives in Florida. I bought her a house and she has a retirement pension."

"You are inviting her to the wedding, but she never called you at the hospital."

"I didn't contact her and asked Uncle Russ not to. She'd just worry and probably have come up. I didn't want her to do either. She's not very able anymore. I called her after I got home and off the narcotics. She scolded me for not letting her know." A faint smile settled on Kyria's face. "I can't wait to see her. She's flying in on Thursday before the wedding. I got a room for her at the Hilton near the interstate. I have a driver hired to bring her to the wedding."

Kyria was relaxed but so passive. As the conversation progressed all her enthusiasm seemed to drain away. It concerned Mark. What was she thinking? Was she just tired from the active weekend? They'd attended worship service that morning. Kyria had enjoyed Hutch's sermon, but had been somewhat uncomfortable as he introduced her to many family friends.

"Haven't you ever had a best friend? Some girl your age you could play dolls with, giggle over stupid stuff, share teenaged angst with?"

"No."

"What about college? I know you got your degree from CSU."

"I lived in our penthouse and had bodyguards who took me everywhere."

"What?"

"My parents were afraid I'd either be kidnapped or some man would sweep me off my feet because they knew we had money. It's been known to happen."

"So basically, I'm your first friend."

"Yes. Now I have two. You and Amisa."

Mark was stunned. Kyria had never had a friend or boyfriend. He'd been her doctor and Amisa was her respite aide. He couldn't imagine not having any friends. Never having the opportunity to make friends. Being kept from interacting with anyone other than those her parents had hired.

"You graduated from college over six years ago. What did you do then? Did you get an apartment and a job?"

Kyria was silent for a few moments. "My parents hired," she made quote marks when she said the word hired, "me to redecorate their properties. They had me live in each one while the work was going on."

"Did you still have bodyguards?"

"Yes. Their families would be moved nearby. They were all married."

It figures. They wouldn't want a bodyguard sweeping their little girl off her feet and marrying her for their money. Mark didn't want to think of the implications to their marriage from her background.

CHAPTER NINETEEN

Kyria didn't go out to purchase a traditional wedding gown. There were plenty of gowns she'd had for the charity galas she'd had to go to with her parents and more recently Uncle Russ. They hung in garment bags in the closet. She'd only worn each one time since it would have been disgraceful to be seen at a second event in a dress she'd worn before, according to her mother.

She sorted through the dresses until she found the one she was thinking of. Traditional white, the gown was a one strap sheath with a bow low on the opposite hip gathering the long flow of the full satin skirt. Sprays of ruby crystals 'held' the bow in place with a large crystal in the center. A curve of the gems ran from the hip up to the shoulder and over onto the back. Then it swirled down and around the skirt, widening, then thinning, coming to a point at the hip bow. Kyria had worn it to a Christmas charity event several years ago. This would be an opportunity to wear it again. There were earrings, a bracelet and pendant necklace which were not crystal but real rubies that she had inherited from her parents.

It was a dress Kyria loved and saved hoping for the opportunity to wear it again. Never had she thought it would become her wedding gown. The evening of their return from Mark's parent's she had taken it out of the closet and hung it on the hook on the wall. In the morning she would try it on hoping she had gained enough weight for it to fit. There was barely enough time to make alterations and it would cost a fortune to have them done in time.

In the morning Kyria called Amisa and asked if she had time to stop by that day. When Kyria had been released from the need for respite care she asked Amisa if she would like to keep coming once a week to help her maintain her apartment. It had worked out for both of them since Kyria did need some help as she was still weak and Amisa could use the extra income.

Today though, it wasn't for Amisa to work, but to allow Kyria to tell her about Mark and invite the nurse and her family to the wedding. She wanted to do this in person. Amisa was more than simply a nurse or employee to Kyria. She was a friend, at least Kyrie hoped so. It was very important to her since she liked the black woman so much.

After Amisa had checked with her husband she called Kyria back. "I talked to Tyron and he'll take the kids to Micky D's so we can have some girl time. I'll be there around four o'clock."

When they finished their call Kyria was excited. Maybe she really could have a friend. Suffering with shyness and not having experience with continuing relationships made her unsure as to how to make and keep friends.

Now she had Mark who was even more than a friend, but she wanted to have a female friend. Her growing up years had been spent with various tutors and moving from place to place, country to country, sometimes with her parents, often not. The only truly constant person in her life had been her nanny, Mamie.

Even when Kyria had gone to college, as she'd told Mark, she wasn't allowed to live in a dorm or with other girls her age. Instead she'd had bodyguards and lived in her parents' penthouse being driven to and from classes by the guards. Once she was in her penthouse in late afternoon the guards had gone home to their families and Kyria had been alone.

Wanting to fit into the college scene she had tried to go to an event without letting her bodyguards know. When Kyria had exited the apartment building she realized she had no idea where to go or how to get there. Always someone had taken her wherever she needed to go. Suddenly terrified, she turned around and fled back to her lonely penthouse. Once settled in the safety of her bedroom she began to reflect.

Never once had she gone anywhere by herself. At least one adult had always been with her and gotten her to her destination. She didn't know how to drive since she had bodyguards who drove. They also took care of every detail when she needed to travel somewhere. At least she knew how to get groceries, even though her 'shadows' were always with her.

Wrapped in bubble wrap. That's what she had been all her life. Protected from life so she wouldn't be broken. Now on the cusp of adulthood Kyria needed to burst free so she could actually live life, not be totally sheltered from it.

Her parents wouldn't allow the removal of her bodyguards and Kyria knew she wasn't equipped to be without them. Instead she began slowly, carefully, to venture out into the world around her apartment building.

The first time she entered the Jimmy John's across from her building without her bodyguards Kyria's stomach was in her throat. Eyes darting left and right waiting for someone to jump on her and throw her into a vehicle. Her hand shook as she pulled her wallet from her purse to pay for her sandwich. With it gripped tightly in her hand she ran back across the street and returned to her apartment. She breathed a sigh of relief when she entered her penthouse.

For the rest of her freshman year and all through the next three Kyria watched, listened and learned to function in the world without someone taking care of every detail for her. The bodyguards didn't leave her alone, but she took over many of the details of life they had been doing for her. Purchasing her airplane tickets, getting herself checked in and through security. Paying the bills which weren't automatically deducted. She even took driving lessons and obtained her license.

None of this was mentioned to her parents. Kyria had spoken with all the bodyguards. Not happy at the start of the conversation, she was able to explain her reasoning and goals convincing them of the wisdom of her intentions.

After getting a soda from the fridge Kyria sat down with her iPad and looked at the list of her tasks for the wedding. She didn't want to disappoint Heather, by not getting her tasks done.

It would be a terrible way to begin the relationship with her mother-in-law.

Nervous about whether she could accomplish everything brought dark times in her past to the surface. She pushed them away. Now was not the time to let them draw her in. Rubbing her hands along the skin under her arms, Kyria focused on each item on her checklist making the calls or scheduling the time to do them.

~~~~~

"Well girl, thanks for the invite for a night out. Even if it's still afternoon." Amisa, with her ever present neon orange bag, gave Kyria a hug as she entered the apartment.

"I have news I want to share with you and want to have time to really chat about it. Come, sit. Would you like a soda?"

"Sure thing." Amisa sat on the couch and kicked her shoes off. "My that feels good. I've been on my feet all day. So what's this news you're wanting to tell me?" Amisa popped the top of the can Kyria handed her as she joined the black woman on the couch.

Kyria couldn't help it. Her smile stretched her face until it began to pull. "Mark and I are getting married."

She held out her left hand that was no longer ringless. Instead there was a large pear shaped diamond surrounded by small pink ones. The band was filled with more white diamonds. When the wedding band was added her finger would sparkle.

"Shut up. No way." Amisa's mouth dropped open and her eyes went wide. She took hold of Kyria's hand and gave a small whistle.

Giggling, Kyria said, "Yes, he asked me two Saturdays ago. Last weekend we went to visit his family."

"So when's the big day?" Amisa said after giving Kyria a big hug. Again Amisa's mouth dropped open when she was told the wedding would be in less than a month. "Shut up. No way you can get a wedding ready in such a short time. Besides, what's the rush?" Amisa's voice deepened. "You aren't in trouble, are you?"

"No. It's because Mark's condo is full of mold. He's living in a cheap motel right now until the wedding. Then we'll live here until the remodel is done." Kyria went on to explain the horrors of Mark's condo, both of them laughing and wondering what type of person had decorated it and what sort of lifestyle they might be living.

After they finished the giggling fit Kyria took Amisa's hand. "Will you stand up with me?"

For the third time in an hour Amisa's mouth made a big 'O'. "You want me to stand up with you? Why? Don't you have some family or close friend?"

Kyria looked down at their clasped hands. "My only family is my brother. I don't know where he is. There's no one I feel closer to than you. Even if you say no, I still want you and your family to come. There are plenty of children for yours to play with. Please?"

Something flitted across Amisa's face before she smiled and said, "I'd love to stand up with you. Can't be your maid of honor since I got three kids, but I can be your matron of honor." She grabbed Kyria and gave her a long hug.

The discussion turned to dresses so they went to the bedroom where Kyria's gown was tried on and exclaimed over. Even though she had gained weight the fit was loose enough that some altering was needed. That would be arranged for tomorrow.

The rest of their time together was spent shopping for a dress for Amisa. The quarrel of who would pay for the dress ended with Kyria winning and taking Amisa to an upscale boutique where they found a flowing sleeveless gown of hand-dyed silk in reds and yellows. A yellow shawl would cover her shoulders if the weather was cool. It would be a dress Amisa could wear over and over.

Convincing Kyria to wear ruby colored shoes didn't take long. Amisa's love of color and quirky style preferences spilling over when they found a sparkly pair. Jokes of clicking the heels together while saying, "There's no place like home, but it's full of mold," even made the sales clerk laugh.

Supper at a tapas restaurant provided the hungry shoppers a chance to review their purchases. One had been a negligee Amisa had convinced the blushing Kyria to buy.

Mark called while they were eating and would meet them at the apartment. He claimed he couldn't go a moment longer not seeing his bride to be. When Kyria told Amisa she grabbed the phone and told him to be patient. They were having their bachelorette party and he needed to sit tight while Kyria finished sowing her wild oats.

It wasn't far into the evening when they arrived back at the apartment to find Mark sitting in the hallway with his back against the door.

"I'm just doing as I was told and sitting tight," Mark said with a grin.

"Oh honey, you need to keep this one. A man who does what he's told," Amisa said.

Once settled in the apartment the excited ladies showed Mark their purchases. All but one. The negligee stayed in the bag. It would be saved until the honeymoon. Kyria didn't show him her wedding gown either. The expression on his face when they showed him the ruby shoes made both ladies laugh.

Amisa headed home saying that Tyron might not be able to get the kids settled for bed, him being too much of a kid himself. She didn't want to have to spend an hour calming her children's excitement before it was bedtime.

~~~~~

As soon as the door closed and they were alone Mark pulled Kyria to him and gave her a big kiss. "So you two had fun and got a lot accomplished?"

Her head resting on his chest Mark felt Kyria smile. "Yes, at least I did and I think Amisa did, too. She's so much fun to be with. I hope she stays my friend."

"Why wouldn't she?"

"I've not had friends before. Not really."

"You've led a pretty lonely life so far. I'm going to make sure that doesn't happen anymore. We'll find a new church and meet new people, and as sweet and wonderful as you are, you'll develop friendships and never have time for your poor old husband."

She let out an amused breath. "Most likely. I'll become the most popular person in town and you'll have to make an appointment just to spend a few moments with me."

He decided to shut her up with a kiss. One led to two then

several more.

Kyria tipped her head back and looked at him. "You need to leave. Temptation is roaring like a lion ready to devour."

Mark was feeling the same way. Silently, he counted the days until the wedding. He gave her a quick kiss on the nose and left the apartment.

CHAPTER TWENTY

Kyria walked into the hospital cafeteria. She was having lunch with Mark. There were so many decisions to be made about the condo renovation, they were planning on going over a number of them during his lunch hour. Time was getting short. They only had two more weeks before the wedding. The condo wouldn't be finished so they planned to stay in her apartment until it was done.

There was an empty table by the wall so she sat down to wait for him. Opening the messenger bag she pulled out her notes and began to sort the various paint chips and fabric samples.

"Well, who have we here? The little bomb victim who seems to have captured the fancy of the most eligible doctor around."

Kyria looked up and saw a very well built blonde whose floral nurse's scrubs were maybe a size too small. They stretched across various places on her body showing off her 'assets.'

"Pardon me?" The nurse wasn't one she was familiar with. She'd never seen her before.

"You won't be able to keep him, you know. You won't be woman enough for him. He's used to so much more woman. He'll get bored with you. You're too inexperienced, too innocent, too bland. He needs a woman with so much more to offer." The nurse shifted her stance slightly displaying herself just a bit more. The message was obvious. Kyria didn't measure up to what the woman had. The inference that she and Mark had a past relationship was evident.

Heat blossomed up Kyria's neck and across her face. She

dropped her eyes and looked at the tabletop covered with ideas for Mark's and her future home. "Thank, thank you for your concern." She had no idea what else to say so she kept silent. She also kept her hands in her lap. No need to display her trembling hands to the woman.

When Kyria didn't respond or look at her again the nurse finally left. Doubts flooded Kyria's mind. The woman was beautiful. Curves in all the right places. Though her hair had been confined in a bun it was definitely shiny, full and wavy. There was no way Kyria could compete with her. She was still too thin, too weak, too just not enough of anything.

No, the nurse was right. There was not a smidgeon of a chance for Mark's interest to remain with her. If they had a past relationship then nothing Kyria could do would keep him from going back. There just wasn't enough of her both physically and otherwise to hold him.

Gathering the papers and fabrics she'd so carefully arranged on the table she stuffed them haphazardly into the messenger bag. Kyria couldn't face him just now. She quickly texted him, then left the cafeteria, never noticing the doctor at another table who had watched the entire exchange frown.

~~~~~

Mark looked at the text totally confused. *Sorry can't make lunch. Also busy tonight. Maybe tomorrow will let you know.* Kyria had never cancelled on him before. He shot her a quick text back asking if anything was wrong.

Since he wasn't having lunch with her he didn't go to the cafeteria. Instead, he simply went to his office to work on reports and signing off on medical records.

When he realized an hour had passed and he hadn't received a reply he texted again. Now, he was worried. She always replied within a few minutes. If not, then he knew she was sleeping. This time she couldn't have been asleep when he texted because she had contacted him first.

Mark tried calling. It went straight to voicemail. She'd turned off her phone? Now he knew something was wrong. She had texted before she left to come to the hospital. He'd just finished and was getting ready to head to the cafeteria to meet her when she'd cancelled. His text had not been responded to and now her phone was turned off. What was going on?

Glancing at his watch, Mark bit off a curse. That showed him he needed to calm himself. He didn't slip into bad language often but supreme stress could trigger it. He had four more hours to his shift.

Four hours later he again bit back a curse. Another doctor had called in sick and he was needed to cover the next eight hours. Now he couldn't even go to her apartment and try to see her. He wouldn't get out of the hospital until well after she was sleeping.

Mark tried to call again and it, again, went straight to voicemail. Something was definitely wrong. Not only was he worried, he was getting angry. They'd promised to talk to each other. Not keep anything from the other. Now she was keeping whatever it was from him. After their discussion about the gossip and him not telling her who would have thought this would happen?

Suddenly it hit him. Whatever had happened had made her doubt. She was trying to hide. Pulling in to tend to the hurt. Protecting herself from further pain.

His anger toward her dissolved. All he wanted to do was pull her into his arms and hold her until she realized how much he loved her and wanted to be where she fled to when she needed comfort and healing.

But he was stuck at the hospital and she'd turned her phone off.

~~~~~

Kyria sat on her sofa, two cats on her lap and a empty box of tissues beside her, used tissues scattered around the wastebasket at the end of the sofa. Her iPad Bible app was open. She'd spent the afternoon and evening reading every verse she could about comfort and trust and security. They'd all given her a measure of peace but doubts and fears assailed her mind.

"Enough," Kyria said as she stood up. Her body protested the movement. She'd been sitting too long. "I'm going to take every thought captive to Christ."

She thought about calling Mark, but felt just a little too fragile at the moment. Turning her phone on she saw that she had four text messages and two voice mails. Reading and listening to them brought more tears to her eyes. He was so concerned about her.

Since he was working she sent him a text saying she was sorry she'd been unavailable for so long and for him not to worry. She was fine. Well, sort of. She would meet him tomorrow for lunch, as they'd planned today, and tell him about it.

He texted right back that he was glad she'd contacted him. Then in all caps, NEVER TURN OFF YOUR PHONE AGAIN.

That made her smile and she pushed her lingering doubt away. She knew it would come back tomorrow, but for now she would bask in the glow of the worry and love evidenced in all those capital letters.

CHAPTER TWENTY-ONE

Kyria stepped into the empty chapel in the hospital. She'd come a bit early so she'd have time to pray and think before she saw Mark. This morning she had woken up again attacked by insecurity, fear and doubt. These were not of God so she really needed to get her head right before she met with him.

The room was softly lit with indirect lighting. Warm golden oak pews with red velvet cushions were in rows with an aisle up the middle. She sat a few rows from the back. There was no cross, testament to its multi-religion usage. Although having one to focus on would have been nice, it wasn't necessary.

Praying for freedom from her fears, Kyria didn't hear the door open.

"Kyria."

She started into awareness and turned looking into the concerned gaze of Nurse Gadsden.

"Are you alright?"

"Did you know I was in here?"

"No, I come here often. I pray for all my patients but when there is a special need I come and pray here. Seems I can focus in the quiet." She gave a gentle smile. "I came here quite often the first few weeks you were in the hospital."

"I never knew. Thank you. That means so much to me."

"So what brings you here today? I wouldn't have thought the hospital chapel was high on your list of places to be less than two weeks before your wedding."

"You know about the wedding?" Kyria was surprised. They

had placed an engagement announcement in the newspaper but since the wedding was to be so small they hadn't really spread the news around.

"Dr. Jenner told me last week. Said he had to tell someone here at work or he'd bust. He asked me not to spread the news as he didn't want some people getting the wrong idea or doing something that might hurt you." Something must have shown on Kyria's face because Nurse Gadsden sat down next to her and placed an arm around her shoulder. "Someone has said something to you. What and who?"

The compassion and caring brought tears to Kyria's eyes. She wiped them away. Too many had been shed in the last day. She took a deep breath and let it out slowly.

"I came to meet Mark for lunch yesterday. While I was waiting for him this nurse came up and said some, well, pretty awful things to me. Told me I wouldn't be enough for him. That he needed more of a woman." Kyria paused. "She inferred that she and Mark had a past relationship that was, umm, extremely close."

"Let me guess," Nurse Gadsden said drily. "Buxom blonde, pretty in an overblown way, her scrubs too tight."

"That's her." Kyria was afraid her doubts would be confirmed.

"She's been after Dr. Jenner for years. He's rebuffed her every time. The last time that I know of he threatened to go to Human Resources and claim sexual harassment."

Kyria's jaw dropped open. "Oh, poor Mark. I suppose I could be angry he hasn't told me, but I'm going to choose not to be."

"Yeah, might be best. I don't think men want to talk about being sexually harassed, probably even more than women do." Nurse Gadsden gave her shoulders a hug. "You've got that man pretty much wrapped around your finger. He was a mess yesterday when he couldn't get a hold of you. He'd check his phone then mumble about someone turning theirs off. He was not a happy camper."

"I got that idea when I turned mine back on and had a bunch of messages."

Her phone pinged and she took it out of her purse. "Mark's wondering where I am. I need to go." She gave the nurse a hug.

"Thank you. God sent you as an angel to me, not only while I was a patient here but today. You're a blessing."

"You are too, honey."

~~~~~

Mark was finishing up in his office before he headed down to the cafeteria to meet with Kyria. His relief had been profound when she'd finally texted him last night. Now he was unsure again. What had caused her behavior? Was it something he did?

"Hey, Mark, you got a minute?" Keith stuck his head in the doorway.

"Sure, a minute. What's up?" Mark was surprised when Keith came in the room and shut the door and sat down in the chair across from his desk.

"I wanted to let you know about something I witnessed yesterday. I know I was pretty crummy to you when you began seeing Kyria. I let myself get caught up in the gossip mill and I'm sorry.

"Anyway, yesterday I was having lunch and Kyria was there. I suppose she was waiting for you." Keith waited for Mark's confirming nod then continued. "Julie walked up to the table and began insinuating that you and she had been an item and that you'd never be faithful to Kyria. That you'd get bored and come back to her."

"What? I've never—"

"I know and you never would. Heck, I don't and I'm the type that might." Keith gave a sad sort of self-deprecating chuckle. "Kyria didn't say much. Just sat there and thanked Julie for her concern. Yeah, I was eavesdropping. My bad. After Julie left your girl sent a text, I'm assuming to you, packed up whatever she'd scattered all over the table and left.

"Knowing women, I figured you might not get what happened out of her. Thought letting you know might help get me back into your good graces. Don't like having you so silent in the OR."

Mark grinned at that. He'd missed their teasing each other during surgery, too. Keith would never be a close friend, their lifestyles and beliefs were too far apart, but as a colleague he was good to work with.

"Hey, thanks. I appreciate your telling me. Kyria's really

special to me." He considered for a moment then said, "I'll let you in on a secret. We're getting married in less than two weeks, and no, that's not the reason. I'll tell you all about it tomorrow during surgery. Don't spread it yet." Mark had an idea how to stop Julie in her tracks and he didn't want Keith stealing his moment. "Need to go now. Meeting Kyria for lunch in the cafeteria."

"Congratulations. I'll keep the news under my hat. Heading that way myself, I'll walk with you."

When Mark arrived he waved Keith off and scanned the room. She wasn't there yet. She'd texted when she left home so she should have been there. That had been early and she hadn't mentioned any errands. Where was she? He texted and was relieved when he got a smiling emoticon in return.

Leaning against a pillar he watched the entry and waited for her to arrive. He'd seen Julie sitting with several other nurses at a table behind him.

When he saw her enter Mark straightened and walked to meet her. Normally, they gave a generic hug, neither comfortable with public displays of affection. Today, however, Mark wrapped his arms around her and gave her a long kiss.

The cafeteria went silent.

Mark turned and faced the room scanning the people there. He wrapped an arm around Kyria holding her close to his side.

"Attention everyone," he called in a loud voice. It carried over the entire cafeteria. "I've got a couple of items I'd like to bring to your attention.

"First, many of you should be ashamed of yourselves for listening to gossip and rumor, believing and spreading it. As medical professionals we're called on to treat the sick and keep the information about a patient confidential.

"Yes, I did stay over at Kyria's one night. She was very ill and unable to stay by herself. Rather than admit her to the hospital when she didn't need it I slept on the couch tending to her medical needs.

"In an effort to comply with HIPPA regulations I stayed quiet about it. Others, including medical professionals who should know better, did not. Conclusions were jumped to and judgments made.

"All I have to say on this is shame on you. If this sort of breach had happened here in the hospital jobs would have been lost. Think about it.

"Second, many of you know Kyria. Well, I'd like you to know one more thing about her." He looked down at her. His eyes searching her face. "She's the love of my life and we are getting married in a couple of weeks."

At first, a solitary set of hands began clapping. It was Keith. Then the room erupted into applause. Several people came forward and congratulated him and hugged her. He knew many had treated her while she was a patient.

Out of the corner of his eye he saw Julie's shocked face as she stood next to her table. Then she stalked off, head held stiffly. He'd speak to her privately letting her know he was aware of her words of the previous day. He'd warn her that if she ever approached or contacted Kyria in any way he was prepared to go to Human Resources with his complaint.

The crowd dissipated, going back to their lunches or to work, leaving Kyria looking at him rather stunned at what he'd done.

"Why did you do that?"

"Because I realized keeping our joy from those I work with was unfair to you. I was trying to wrap you in bubble wrap again hoping to protect you from the gossip going on around here. It didn't work. Julie got to you, anyway. Yes, I know. A friend saw what happened and told me. I appreciate it. Made me pop all those bubbles and unwrap you. You deserve to be hailed as my love and my future wife. The world needed to know. At least this little part of it.

"I also wanted to let them wallow in their shame. It probably wasn't too nice of me but it needed to be said. Now they can believe what they want. I don't care. They've been told the truth. You can handle whatever they say or do. You're strong and capable enough." He pulled her toward the serving line. "Come on. I've got a huge appetite all of a sudden. I haven't eaten since breakfast yesterday. Too upset to eat."

Kyria stopped. "Thank you. I love you, too." She gave him a quick kiss on the lips. "Let's eat."

~~~~~

Later that evening, after they had talked over everything Mark fell asleep. Kyria stood by the sofa he was lying on, wishing she could just let him lie there. Soon she thought. No, then she'd still wake him up enough to move him to the bedroom, but not yet. She was counting the days.

Gently she shook his shoulder. "Mark, honey, you need to wake up and go home."

"Can't," he mumbled. "Mold."

She chuckled. He was right. He couldn't go home. The condo was torn up with the remodel.

"Well, you can't stay here. We got in enough trouble the last time that happened. Don't want a repeat of that." She shook his shoulder again.

He opened one eye and looked at her. "Five minutes, Mom?" He sounded like a teenager begging for a few more minutes before he started his day.

"Nope, get up and get out of here. I need to sleep and you can't do that here yet." She stepped back as he began to stretch.

"One of these days. You won't be kicking me out." He grinned at her.

"Ten days, not counting the honeymoon since we won't be here then." She smiled back at her.

Mark stood and grabbed her around the waist. "I can't wait." He kissed her, leaving them both panting. "Now, I need to get out of here before…" He left the sentence hanging. They both knew, felt what might happen.

He gave her one more kiss then pulled his car keys out of his pocket. "You know. I really hate that motel I'm staying at. Can't wait until next Tuesday when we leave for my folks."

Kyria reached a hand out and touched his chest sliding her fingers across the fabric of his golf shirt. "I can't wait either. Now go."

CHAPTER TWENTY-TWO

On Tuesday before the wedding, Kyria was finishing packing what she would wear the rest of the week as well as the type of clothing Mark had asked her to pack for their honeymoon. He was keeping the destination secret but she had a feeling they would be going to the Caribbean since he'd told her to pack bathing suits and summer clothes and be sure to bring her passport.

A knock on her front door brought a smile and Kyria hurrying to answer it since she was expecting Mark. They were heading to his parents' for the rest of the week. A key to her apartment for him had been gotten from the landlord but Mark wasn't going to use it until after the wedding.

Her jaw dropped when she saw who was standing there. "Turner! What are you doing here?"

"Aren't you going to invite me in, sis?"

"Of course." Kyria stepped aside and Turner stormed past into the center of her living room.

"So, Kyria, what's this I hear about you getting married?"

"Yes, I'm getting married on Saturday. How have you been?" Kyria didn't like his tone and wasn't going to take any guff from him. Turner hadn't been evident in her life since the death of their parents and barely there before.

"Cut the crap, Kyria. I want to know about this guy and how he's wormed his way into your confidence to get at your trust fund."

"First, you will be polite and respectful to me and my choices.

Second, no one has wormed their way to get my trust. Third, you have a tremendous amount of gall coming and throwing your weight around when I've not heard from you in I don't know how many months."

"A lot you know. You've been sheltered for all your life. What do you know of conmen?" Turner's voice rose until he was nearly yelling.

Kyria tried to keep her voice calm and quiet but in her anger at her brother's contempt for her abilities as well as his lack of being a part of her life she failed. "Turner, you've lost the right to comment on my life. You have no clue as to who I am or what my capabilities are. I'm not as stupid as you think. Maybe if you had been around or even contacted me occasionally you'd know more about me."

"I've been busy."

"Right," she shouted back at him.

~~~~~

Mark heard the yelling as he exited the elevator. Running toward Kyria's apartment, he pulled out his keys and fumbled finding the right one. With no hesitation, he unlocked the door and rushed in.

"Kyria, are you all right? Is this man bothering you?"

"Mark." He could hear the relief in her voice. She ran to him so he wrapped an arm around her waist drawing close to his side. "This is my brother, Turner. He seems to think I'm incapable of managing my life and that you are a conman intent on fleecing me of my money."

Being polite, Mark offered his hand to Turner to shake. There was a pause before it was grudgingly taken.

The familial resemblance was there. The same green eyes and light brown hair. His was a bit on the long side and there was a scruff of a beard as if he hadn't shaved in a few days. His clothing was simply a polo shirt and khaki pants but of a high end brand. It was his stance that Mark noted. It was hostile, almost as if he was ready to fight."Nice to meet you, Turner. I'm Mark Jenner."

"So, what do you do for a living?"

Mark smiled. "I'm a doctor. A hospitalist and surgeon. I took care of Kyria while she was in the hospital." He seated Kyria on the couch and sat next to her, placing his arm on the back behind her. Turner sat in a chair across the coffee table from them.

"What?" Turner exclaimed. "When were you in the hospital?" He'd turned his gaze to look at his sister.

"I was there for about two months after the explosion at the building where I work." Kyria's tone was a mix of irritation and disinterest. "Mark, would you like something to drink?"

"Sure, honey, the usual." Mark wondered if she would ask her brother. She was indeed angry at him.

As Kyria stood and headed into the kitchen she said over her shoulder, "Turner, would you like a Coke?"

The look of surprise on Turner's face amused Mark. He figured the man didn't have a clue as to what Kyria might drink and wouldn't have thought she would know his preference.

"Uh, sure."

"So, what brings you here, Turner?" Mark asked, knowing the answer already.

"Uncle Russ emailed me about the wedding. I felt that I needed to come. Kyria doesn't have much life experience. But what's this about her being in the hospital?"

"Kyria was leaving work when a terrorist bomb went off in the lobby. The force threw her into and over a parking meter and onto the windshield of the truck parked there. She was gravely injured and spent nearly two months, like she said, in the hospital where I work. I was the doctor who cared for her during that time."

"That's when you found out she was wealthy, right?"

Mark chose to ignore the animosity. "No, I only knew she didn't have any family who cared enough to come or call."

"I didn't know."

"And never tried to get in touch with her simply because she's your only family. Didn't bother to make sure she knew where you were or how to contact you either."

Kyria entered carrying a tray with the drinks on it. Mark stood and took the tray from her and set it on the coffee table. An awkward silence descended as the glasses were distributed. Finally Kyria broke it.

"So Turner. Just what do you want? Why are you here? Just to make trouble for me or because you really care?"

Turner stiffened. "I care Kyria. You're my little sister. I want to make sure you don't get swindled."

"Such faith you have in me. I'm truly touched. My brother cares enough about my money to come when he feels it's threatened, but not enough to make sure I can contact him when I'm fighting for my life."

Turner's face became red. His bravado left him and he slumped back in his chair. "You're right. I don't have the right to object. I've been a pretty lousy brother, haven't I?"

"In a word, yes."

Mark stayed silent. This was the time for Kyria and Turner to reconcile. He sent up a prayer this would be a new start for their relationship. As close as he was to his siblings and parents, Mark couldn't understand not contacting them each by phone or email at a minimum of once a week. He especially wanted Kyria to develop a positive relationship with her brother.

"I have no excuse except selfishness. Doing my own thing. I just never took the time to think about you not being able to contact me. I won't do that again, I promise."

"Thank you."

Mark could tell by the tone of her voice Kyria didn't believe Turner would follow through.

"Um, Mark said you were pretty badly hurt."

"Yes, I nearly died and was in a coma for, how long Mark?"

"Ten days. We kept her under because of the pain she would be in. Even after we brought her out she was still in terrible pain." Mark set his glass on the table and took hold of her free hand. He saw Turner's look. Hopefully, as they talked, now that the emotions were spent, all the doubts Turner had could be eased.

"When I got the email from Uncle Russ he mentioned you had been in the hospital. He told me about your upcoming wedding at the same time. Why didn't he let me know when you were injured?"

Kyria explained about the lawyer being out of the country and how Mark had found out who her emergency contact was. She told of Mark's continuing contact after her release from the hospital. No mention was made of her overdose on the pain killers.

"Usually, it's the patient falling in love with the doctor. This time it was the reverse, I fell in love with Kyria." When she looked at him the light in her eyes lit up his heart. Man, he couldn't wait until Saturday.

"Just to ease your worry, Turner," Kyria said. "Mark didn't know anything about my trust until we were signing prenups."

That obviously surprised Turner. "So he didn't mind when you brought up a prenup?"

"Nope. He wanted one, too."

"My family owns Jenner Construction and each of my siblings had prenups. I was going to bring it up for her to sign, not knowing Kyria would have one for me to sign, too. She mentioned it first."

"See, brother, I'm not as naive as you think I am."

"So how did he think you supported yourself?"

"I work. I was leaving work when the explosion happened. Didn't you hear that?"

"I figured it was some charity you volunteered for. Why would you need to work?"

"I enjoy it and I like living within what I make. Not that I never dip into my savings. Usually, it's for donating or giving gifts to those I think are worthy."

Turner seemed confused.

"I know you don't understand. I could never work and probably never touch the principle of the trust, let alone the savings I have from my earnings. I guess I want the challenge of my work and want to be around people who don't know that I don't have to. People are more, I don't know, real I guess, when they don't know you're filthy rich."

"What are you doing for work?" Turner looked and sounded curious, almost as if he couldn't image Kyria working at all.

"At the moment, I'm still on leave, but will go back after our honeymoon. I work for Kempfer Decorating. They've been very understanding of my being gone so long."

"When I contacted their HR man to find Kyria's emergency

contact, he assured me she would be welcomed back whenever she wanted. She's considered one of the rising stars of the company." Mark squeezed her hand.

"Oh."

"Turner, I'm twenty-seven years old and have been living and managing quite well since I've been on my own. I'm perfectly capable of dealing with life and all its challenges without you swooping in when you hear a tidbit about me from Uncle Russ. Does he know you're in town, by the way?"

"Well, no. I came straight here from the airport. You wouldn't want to put me up would you? It would be a good time for us to catch up." Turner gave a sheepish grin.

"No, you can afford a hotel. There are several that meet your standards in the city."

"Besides, we're leaving for my folks' as soon as we can get Kyria's luggage in the car. We won't be back for ten days. We have the wedding on Saturday then a week honeymoon," Mark said.

"Oh."

When Kyria didn't say anything, Mark squeezed her hand. "Turner, would you please come to the wedding? Uncle Russ is giving me away."

Mark noticed she didn't offer to change those plans and ask her brother to do the honors. "Yes, please come, Turner. We'd love to have you. One more person won't make a difference. You can even bring a date if you want."

~~~~~

After Turner agreed, and got directions and the name of the hotel the out of town guests would be staying in, he left. When the door was shut behind him Kyria slumped against it.

"I was so surprised when it was him standing there. I thought it was you. Then he started railing at me about me being suckered by some conman. He made me so mad. He hasn't bothered to keep in touch for three years then he thinks he can walk in here and…"

Mark put his fingers on her lips stopping the tirade that was building within her. "Shhh. It's all over." He wrapped his arms around her and pulled her against his chest. "Turner understands

145

now and won't cause any trouble. I'm sure he'll meet with your Uncle Russ and get more details from him." He laughed. "I could hear you guys yelling at each other when the elevator doors opened. My key works, by the way. I didn't want to wait to get to you if you were in danger from someone."

Kyria took a deep breath and straightened. "I'm almost ready to head out. Just a few things to pack. If Turner hadn't shown up we'd be on the road now."

"I'll wash the glasses while you do that. Then we'll be off to get married. I don't know about you, but I can't wait."

"I suppose it's okay. Just another day in the life of this stuck up snob." Kyria imitated a bored socialite, a familiar persona in the circles her parents had occupied.

"You go on now." Mark picked up a cloth napkin from the tray of glasses and snapped her on the bottom with it as she headed to the bedroom eliciting a short squeal. Kyria grinned as she threw the last few items into her smallest suitcase. She was as anxious for Saturday to arrive as Mark was.

CHAPTER TWENTY-THREE

"Go away Mark. The rehearsal and dinner are over and it's time to say goodnight to your bride. You'll see her when she walks down the aisle tomorrow." Chloe, Mark's sister, was pushing him away from Kyria. Mark was staying at Hutch and Chloe's house tonight.

The entire family had come back to the Jenner parents' home from the restaurant where the rehearsal dinner had been held. All except the children of Mark's siblings. They had been excluded from the entire affair. None of them were in the wedding so there was no need for them to be around. Mark's father, Will, had declared that the natives would be restless the entire evening and they could just be restless at home instead of at the expensive restaurant where they would eat not even a third of the costly meals they'd be served.

"Well, let me at least say good-bye to her." Mark looked over his sister's head and saw Kyria laughing at their antics. "Are you sure you don't want to elope tonight? We have the license. We could find a justice of the peace or a judge who'd do the honors? Or hey, Hutch could do the honors right here, right now."

"And deprive your sister of the chance to boss you around? No way. Besides, I'd never disappoint your mother after all the work she's gone to for us."

"All the work she's gone to?" exclaimed Luke, Mark's older brother. "I didn't see her carrying tables and chairs and I don't know what all down to the pond and setting them up in neat rows. Did you know there's a certain distance chairs are supposed to be set apart so the people won't feel too crowded?"

"Not far enough in most cases," Gavin groused. "I've sat pressed up against too many people, too many times. I'd have put them at least a foot apart, but my dear wife wouldn't let me."

Mark had made his way around the milling family members and gotten next to Kyria. He put his arm around her shoulders and gave her a hug. "How about you and I go inspect the chair setup to be sure they are the proper distance apart?" He had whispered the words into her ear. She giggled.

Heather clapped her hands. "I'll give you five minutes on the front porch. Then you are leaving, along with my other children and their spouses, and I'm going to tuck Kyria into bed. You want her to look her best tomorrow don't you?" She gave all those who no longer lived at this address a look that said, you will listen and obey. Good natured grumbling accompanied the grouping into couples as they prepared to leave.

Mark, wanting to take advantage of the bustling, took Kyria's hand and pulled her outside and along the porch to the darker end where a light was burned out. "Are you as ready as I am for tomorrow?" Mark asked as he wrapped her in his arms. He barely waited for her affirmative reply before his lips captured hers.

~~~~~

"You look wonderful, my dear."

Kyria looked at Heather's face in the mirror as they stood together after pinning the red crystal tiara in the veil covering her face.

"Thank you for all your help. I couldn't have done this without all you Jenner women."

"You'll be a Jenner woman in just a little while, and I'm so glad you are. Mark is so...I don't know...settled I guess is the word. It's as if you complete him in some way."

Kyria knew just what Heather was saying. She felt the same way. Mark filled a part of her she hadn't even known was empty. She would do whatever she could to be the wife he wanted and needed.

"It's almost time. I'll find Mr. Naylor and send him to escort you. Amisa is just outside." Heather came to stand in front of

Kyria. She took hold of the bride's hands, smiled and said, "Welcome to the family."

Tears filled Kyria's eyes. She felt more accepted by this lovely woman than she ever had by her parents. Each one of the Jenner family had embraced her as one of them the weekend she and Mark had visited. Though she tried, Kyria couldn't speak past the lump in her throat blinking in an attempt to control her tears.

"None of that now," Heather said, waving her own hand in front of her face. "You'll smear your makeup and possibly mine. We'd have to postpone the ceremony until we could redo it. Mark wouldn't appreciate his mother causing his to bride cry and him to wait to make her his wife."

Kyria laughed and accepted the tissue Heather handed her. "He does get grumpy when he has to wait. He's always early, too."

"So I'll get your uncle and we'll start this wedding at least five minutes before time."

~~~~~

Mark stood next to his brother Gavin, his best man. With Kyria having only Amisa standing up with her the brothers had drawn straws. Gavin lost. Now clothed in tuxedos, they waited for the music to change indicating the ladies were about to appear.

The inability to decide whether the butterflies attacking the lining of his stomach were from fear or excitement changed the moment Kyria stepped from the shadow of the covered patio into the sunlight. Mark had never seen her look so beautiful. As she approached he felt his grin widen into a smile knowing he looked like a love-sick fool but didn't care. He knew how close she had come to dying and him not ever having had the opportunity to know and love her.

Mark watched her follow Amisa and walk beside Russell Naylor between the chairs filled with their guests. Kyria's expression changed from nervous anxiety slowly to gladness then joy when she reached him. Extending his hand, Russ placed hers into his. It was trembling so he wrapped his fingers around it, bringing it to his lips for a soft kiss as they turned to face the guests. Hutch stepped in front of them and began the ceremony.

The unusual positioning had been at Heather's insistence. She had argued that she wanted to see the face of her last child to marry as he said his vows rather than the back of his head. Not caring one way or another, Mark let Kyria argue with his mother figuring she would. Instead, she had indicated it made no difference to her. If it meant so much to Heather then they would of course stand facing the audience. Now they stood looking at not only Hutch but also those who had come to celebrate with them.

As soon as Hutch began speaking Mark forgot all about those watching and focused on Kyria. His bride. Mark had begun to put aside the idea he would find a woman he would love. Figuring if he wanted to be married he would have to simply find someone he was attracted to and settle for a comfortable marriage. Kyria's gentle spirit mixed with her quick wit and humor put paid to that thought.

As Mark watched Kyria's face, focusing on her deep green eyes, he lost track of what Hutch was saying until doubt flashed in her eyes followed by humor as she squeezed his hands hard.

"I will? I do?" Mark had no clue which he was supposed to say so he said both. The guests as well as Kyria, Amisa, Gavin and Hutch started laughing. A blush flared across his face then he laughed at himself along with the rest.

"If you'll pay a little attention to me instead of drowning in your bride's eyes we'll get this finished so you can finally kiss her," Hutch said bringing his mirth under control. "You say 'I will' even though you don't have a clue as to what you are agreeing to."

"I will."

Mark noticed that Kyria was relaxed now and smiling a true smile rather than a scared, happy, nervous, excited one. He remembered Hutch saying each ceremony had some moment which broke the tension, usually with humor. It seemed his inattention had accomplished it.

With Mark now focused on what Hutch was saying he didn't miss anymore cues and finally the words he had been waiting for came.

"I now pronounce you man and wife. You may kiss your bride."

Not hesitating a moment Mark pulled Kyria close, said, "I love you," and kissed her long on the lips. He didn't let her go until Hutch cleared his throat.

At least the ceremony was over. Now all he had to do was figure out how long they had to stay at the reception before they headed back to the city. He'd booked the honeymoon suite at the Hilton. It would be a short night since they had to leave for the airport by five o'clock in the morning. He knew Kyria would take longer than he to get ready and also knew sleep was going to be much less than they each normally got.

Rather than a receiving line they greeted each guest as they moved down the aisle. As soon as the family members were hugged each one had an assigned task. The food was catered, but there were still things needing to be attended to.

At last, all the guests had been welcomed so Mark and Kyria headed into the house followed by Hutch, Gavin and Amisa. They would all sign the marriage license, then leave the newly wed couple alone for a while. It was something Mark had insisted upon. He wanted to be sure Kyria wasn't overdoing because of the stress of the day. That was the excuse he gave everyone. The real reason was so he could have some time to give her more kisses before they took on the people and activities of the reception.

~~~~~

Mark picked up her wrist pressing his fingers to Kyria's pulse and looked at his watch. "Your pulse is a little high. What do you suppose brought that on?" He lifted his eyebrow, gazing down at her since he was standing very close.

"I don't know. You're the physician. What do you think caused this?"

"Has today been one charged with emotion?"

"I suppose you could say so." Kyria walked her fingers up the red vest he wore under the tux jacket.

"In what way?" Mark leaned his forehead onto hers.

"Well, I just married the man I love." She was whispering now.

Mark whispered back. "Is that so? How about you kiss him to show him you do?"

Kyria wrapped her arms around his neck and pulled his head

down, lifting her lips to meet his. Nothing more was said for several moments. Then Mark gently pushed her back just a bit.

"This is the last time I'm going to say this. We need to stop. Right now we have a boat load of guests waiting to wish us well. Soon we'll be able to leave and —" He grinned at her. "We won't have to rein in our desires anymore."

"Well, if you want to on get to that activity we've got leave this room and enjoy the boat load of guests. They won't go away or let us leave until we do. Besides, there are two kinds of cake and I want some of both." Kyria gave him another quick kiss and, taking his hand, pulled him out the door.

A note from Sophie

I hope you enjoyed **Mold and Marriage**. Please take a moment to leave a review on Amazon. For independently publishing authors like myself, the reviews are extremely valuable in getting our work noticed. If you take just a few minutes you could help someone else find their next favorite book.

FREE Short Story when you sign up for my newsletter.

Did you like Keith Austin? I did. He had some growth during the book. I liked him so much he's going to get his own book. Since I don't want his love story to be when he comes to know Jesus Christ as his savior I wrote a short story titled **Keith's Coming**. It's free when you sign up for my newsletter. Or if the link doesn't work copy and paste this http://dl.bookfunnel.com/4pu6ns1txb

The newsletter only comes to you when there is actual real, news about my books. You need not worry that your information will ever be released to anyone in any way for anything. I hate spam as much as you do.

Thank you.

Sophie

Books By Sophie Dawson

Cottonwood Series

Healing Love

Lord's Love

Giving Love

Redeeming Love (With George McVey)

Stones Creek Series

Leah's Peace

Chasing Norie

Chloe's Choice (Short Story)

Chloe's Sanctuary

Single Books

Seeing The Life

Rescued By Love (Novelette)

If you enjoyed this book and would like to find other great Christian Indie Authors reads, follow the link below. Christian Books in Multiple Genres, Join Christian Indie Author ~ Readers Group on Facebook. Opportunities for free books and giveaways.

https://www.facebook.com/groups/291215317668431/

www.ingramcontent.com/pod-product-compliance
Lightning Source LLC
Chambersburg PA
CBHW070331130626
46556CB00007B/2810